DEC 1 9 2013

FLUFFERS, INC.

Fluffers, Inc.

A Novel by
Hank Edwards

Lethe Press
Maple Shade, NJ

Copyright © 2002, 2009 Hank Edwards. All rights reserved. No part of this book may be reproduced, stored in retrieval system, or transmitted in any form, by any means, including mechanical, electronic, photocopying, recording or otherwise, without prior written permission of the author.

Originally published by Alyson Books in 2002.

This Lethe Press edition released in 2009.

Lethe Press, 118 Heritage Ave, Maple Shade, NJ 08052

www.lethepressbooks.com   lethepress@aol.com

Printed in the United States of America

Book Design by Toby Johnson

Cover Design by Denny Upkins

ISBN 1-59021-044-1   978-1-59021-044-4

*For Phred,
the man who has helped me to
grow in, oh, so many ways*

1

A Farm Fresh Egg

Kinitia Jones was on a frenzied, over the top phone call when he walked in the door of her company. She eyed him up and down, taking stock of the faded jeans, flannel shirt, and shit kicker boots. He had shaggy blond hair, blue eyes, an 'aw shucks' grin, and extremely white teeth. He looked like he had just stepped out of a Farmer's Weekly magazine layout. She raised a single, exquisitely manicured finger and flicked her eyes away from his wholesome face as she listened to the director on the other end of the line continue to scream at her.

Unable to take it any longer, Kinitia sat back and interrupted the tired old bitch. "Cedric," she said with just a touch of edge in her voice. It wasn't much of an edge, but it stopped the hysterical man in his tracks.

"What?" he snapped.

"In the past, what has the quality of my staff been like?" Kinitia asked.

"That's not the point here, Ms. Jones," Cedric started in again and she once more cut him off.

"Cedric, I think you and I can both agree that my staff is more than able to handle any job you throw at them. How many have gone on to become stars in their own right? More than I can count, I can tell you that." She glanced at the new arrival and rolled her eyes. He smiled back at her, his white teeth lighting up the room.

"All right, I see where you're headed," the director relented. "Just make sure the next one knows what he's doing, for Christ's sake! This last one couldn't keep a plank of aged mahogany stiff."

And with that, the man hung up. Kinitia replaced the receiver, resting her hand on the warm handle for a moment as she pulled together her composure. Then she looked up and smiled. "Hi there. Welcome to Fluffers, Inc. What can I do for you?"

"Well," the young man said with a fast blush pinking his cheeks. "I'm looking for a job."

Kinitia raised a single, impeccable eyebrow. "A job? Here?" He nodded enthusiastically. "Do you know what it is exactly that I hire people to do here?"

"I believe so," he said nervously.

"Okay," she sat back and steepled her fingers beneath her chin. "Enlighten me."

"You loan out men and women to the porn studios to provide a service to the stars between takes to keep them hard or, in the case of women, keep their, uh, well, their . . ."

He faltered and she offered up the word: "Clitoris?"

Another blush and a grateful nod. "Yeah. That. To keep that area stimulated." He paused and fidgeted a little. "Is that right?"

Kinitia nodded, eyeing him with narrowed lids. "It's right. I'm just curious why you think you would be good at this particular endeavor."

"Well, um . . ." he looked around then leaned forward and said quietly. "I really like to suck cock."

Both eyebrows went up this time. "Really? Well, Farm Boy, get in line. Everybody likes to suck cock. Why do you think you are so gifted you can keep a porn star, a man who has made it with hundreds upon hundreds of attractive men, up and ready to go for his next scene?"

He shrugged. "No complaints so far."

Kinitia laughed. Threw back her head and let out a deep, feel good laugh. The kid was honest, she had to give him that. And talk about fresh from the farm! Like her grandma had said on more than one occasion, this one was going to sizzle like crazy when he hit the griddle. She stifled her good humor and gave him a stern look. "I don't tolerate drugs, drunks or thieves."

He nodded. "Neither do I."

"Good. Okay, I'll give you a try. You're paid by the job, not on an hourly basis, got it? So don't milk a job just to get more money." She picked up the phone and pressed a button. "Ken, come up front please. We have a trainee." Kinitia hung up and looked at him. "What's your name, Farm Boy?"

"Charlie Heggensford, ma'am." He stuck out his hand and she smiled as she shook it.

"Charlie, I'm Kinitia Jones. I own, manage, and take pride in my company. I started Fluffers, Inc. about six years ago and have become known in the Los Angeles area as a supplier of quality fluffers. There are two other companies trying to knock me out of business, both run by nasty, degenerate men I won't talk about now, but so far I've been able to maintain my business with respect and determination." She nodded once and Charlie nodded back. "And one more thing . . ."

"Yes?"

"Don't fuck with me," Kinitia warned with a cool smile. "I don't take kindly to being fucked with."

Charlie nodded, his eyes a little wider. "Yes ma'am."

Ken Carlton appeared at the front desk, his dark wavy hair combed to perfection and his T-shirt hugging a muscular upper body. "Hey Kinitia." He turned his eyes to take in Charlie. "Fresh meat, huh?"

"He needs a tour and a few lessons." Kinitia raised her eyebrows. "He's a nice boy, so be nice to him."

"You got it." Ken stuck out a hand. "Ken Carlton, senior fluffer."

"Charlie Heggensford." They shook and then Charlie followed Ken down a long, narrow hallway to a large, open back room. Four leather couches, several chairs, tables with stacks of magazines ranging from Architectural Digest to graphic porn, and three TV sets made up the room. A wet bar took up one wall, stocked with soft drinks and bottled water plus bowls of fresh fruit. Charlie looked around in awe.

"This is nice," he said.

"Yeah, Kinitia takes care of us." Ken introduced him to the twenty other people in the room, six women thrown in among the majority of men. All of them were attractive and in stellar shape. A group of men were watching a gay porn movie. Three of the women were watching a lesbian porn movie, and the rest were watching *Steel Magnolias*.

"So," Ken said as he showed Charlie where the rest rooms were located. "Where are you from?"

"Idaho," Charlie replied and nodded as Ken laughed. "I get that a lot. It's not so bad. My father owns a pretty big farm and ranch outside of a small town in the northern area of the state, not far from some national forests. I liked the town and the land, but I just had to move here to LA to see what all the fuss is about." Charlie shrugged. "I've been here two weeks and lost three jobs."

"What have you tried?" Ken sat on a counter in the bathroom and adjusted his prominent package.

"Waiter, bus boy, valet," Charlie winced at the memories. "Wasn't very good at any of them. So I decided to try my hand at this. I've heard about fluffers, even rented some movies about them, and I got to suck a lot of dick back on the farm."

"Really?" Ken said with surprise. "In Idaho?"

"Sure. You'd be amazed how many men like to get sucked off by a guy. I used to love the harvest season because my Dad would hire more farm hands to help out and they were always hot, hung, and horny." Charlie wet his lips thinking about the men he had serviced in the barn.

"Damn, sounds hot." Ken rubbed his expanding crotch and asked, "Care to give me a demonstration?"

Charlie smiled slightly. "Glad to." He knelt before Ken and slowly unzipped his jeans, pulling them down to the man's ankles. The steadily lengthening cock sprung out as Charlie lowered Ken's boxer briefs and he deftly caught it in his mouth. Ken was long and thick, almost eight inches. His skin tasted salty as if he had swum in the ocean before coming into work and Charlie closed his eyes as the man's dick filled his mouth and eased down his throat. He wrapped his tongue around the bulging shaft, caressing him with his tongue.

"Oh, that's good, Charlie," Ken whispered. "Yeah, just suck gently on it. Oh yeah."

Ken's hips started to pump slowly, slipping his cock out of Charlie's mouth and back in again. His dark, wiry pubic hair brushed up against Charlie's nose and upper lip as his balls swung forward and batted against his chin.

Charlie moved back and focused his suction on the ridge at the base of Ken's head, slurping and sucking on the sensitive mushroom cap of velvet skin. Pre cum leaked out of the piss slit, encouraging Charlie to dip the very tip of his tongue into it. The salty taste of Ken's pre cum coated his tongue as Charlie reached down and worked his jeans open to release his own stiffening boner.

"Oh, that's it baby," Ken whispered. "Get that tongue up in that piss slit. Oh yeah." He let Charlie work the head of his cock for a few more minutes, then began pumping into his face, the speed of his hips quickening until he was all out fucking Charlie's mouth.

"You've got a hot fuckin' mouth there, Charlie," Ken grunted. "I like how you suck cock."

Charlie groaned around the friction of Ken's cock, the taste of the man filling his mouth and the tangy smell of his sweat working up into his nostrils. He worked his fist along his own prick, the head covered with a slick of pre cum that helped lubricate the shaft.

"Oh, fuck, man," Ken gasped. "I'm going to cum." He pulled his cock from between Charlie's bruised lips and stroked himself to orgasm. Big, wet shots of hot cum burst from Ken's dick and splattered across Charlie's face. Blast after blast of cum soaked his forehead, cheeks, and jaw as Ken spent himself.

"Oh, uh, uh," Charlie grunted, his lips parting in the mess of Ken's load as he stood up and came onto Ken's belly and cock. The white, sticky load coated his new friend's hairy belly and groin and dripped from his cock.

"Fuck, man," Ken said, reaching out to steady himself on Charlie's shoulder. "That was fucking hot."

Charlie grinned, feeling the cum already drying on his face. "Yeah it was."

12

They cleaned up at the sink and headed out to the waiting area. Two of the women were gone and Charlie noticed that some of the men were missing as well.

"Guess some calls came in during your first lesson," Ken said and clapped Charlie on the back.

They joined the group watching *Steel Magnolias* and just as Julia Roberts was dying, Kinitia's voice crackled over the intercom. "I need two fluffers at the set of *Lesbian Lap Dance* ASAP."

The men all wrinkled their noses in distaste as the remaining women got up and left the room. Charlie talked with several of the other men, amazed at the fine contours of their faces and perfect bodies visible through their tight clothing. One by one they were all sent off on assignment until Charlie and one other young man were left.

Kinitia appeared in the door to the room and fixed Charlie with a look. "I need someone at the set of *Gone In 60 Suckass*. This director is my most troublesome client and I can't have another problem on his set. Think you can do it?"

Charlie nodded and stood up, butterflies in his stomach. "I won't let you down."

Kinitia smiled and handed him an address and a fifty dollar bill. "They're shooting in some huge house in the hills. Take a cab and afterwards have some lunch on me."

Charlie almost sprinted out of the office and down the hall to the elevator. He hailed a cab and bounced his leg nervously until the car pulled up in front of a large, rambling house. A young, very pretty houseboy wearing only a jockstrap admitted him.

"They're out by the pool," the houseboy said with a dazzling smile. Charlie walked through many rooms and out a wide patio door onto the deck of a sparkling blue pool. Off to the side a large, sweaty man was shouting at two naked, bronze gods as they writhed on mats in the bright sunlight. Both men had perfectly sculpted bodies and big, bulky cocks. Their balls hung heavy between their muscular thighs as they kissed and groped each other. The director told them where to touch and what to lick and suck while the cameraman beside him captured it all on tape.

Charlie watched the scene before him with interest and a little awe. This was the first time he had ever watched men have sex without a VCR and a porn video smuggled into his bedroom. The action unfolding poolside got him instantly aroused. The men had positioned themselves into a 69, each of them swallowing the big, thick cock in their face with an expertise that made Charlie envious. The man on top was broad and hairy with short, dark hair and a trim goatee, his body coated with a layer of glistening sweat. His dark, hairy fingers were gripping the other actor's cock tightly at the base as he took it into his throat to the root.

The man lying on his back adjusted his position and planted his feet flat on the mat beneath him, lifting his hips slightly. He had a smooth, muscular chest with a pierced left nipple and wore his sun-bleached hair in a shaggy surfer cut. His eyes were closed and his hands had reached out to grab either cheek of his partner's ass, kneading the tanned, sweaty globes as he raised and lowered his head to suck the man's cock. When he raised his head and swallowed the thick, tanned cock above him, his partner's shaved, low hanging balls spread out over the bridge of his nose and eyes.

With a grunt, the man on top pulled his blond partner's legs up, shifting his position to be able to get his hands at the actor's asshole. All the time he was manipulating the man beneath him and his position, the actor beneath him kept sucking his cick, a testament to his professionalism.

"That's it, Mike," the director said. "Raise his legs and give us a shot of his hole. Steven, keep sucking his dick, I need good length on that, and then move back to eat Mike's ass."

Mike, obviously the dark haired man on top, began sucking with renewed energy. He moaned now and then around his mouthful of hot, salty cock as his dark fingers began to rub at Steven's sweaty, pink hole. Steven grunted up into Mike's bush while the man massaged his asshole and slid his own fingers back to the sweaty crack of Mike's ass.

Mike released Steven's cock and set to work on the blond man's shaved balls. He sucked at the loose skin and covered it with his wide, pink tongue before taking both testicles into his mouth. All the time he worked Steven's balls, Mike kept rubbing the man's

14

asshole, now and then slipping a finger into the pink hole and bringing it back out again. Steven released Mike's cock from his mouth and reached down to push against the backs of Mike's thighs, encouraging him to slide up. Mike moved up and brought his asshole down directly over Steven's mouth. The blond actor reached up to spread his partner's ass cheeks and then set to work, licking and slurping at Mike's dark ring of muscle. His fingers dug into the fleshy mounds of Mike's cheeks and opened the threshold of his ass even further, allowing Steven to get his tongue deep into Mike's sphincter.

Mike let Steven's balls drop from his mouth and raised his face, closing his eyes and saying, "Oh, yeah. Eat that asshole. Get your tongue up inside me. Fuck me with your tongue. Yeah, that's it." He allowed himself the pleasure of riding Steven's tongue for a short time, then reached down and hauled the blond actor's hips up into the air. He tucked the man's legs beneath his arms and set to work rimming Steven's asshole with abandon. His wide, wet tongue poked at and licked along the pulsing pucker of Steven's hole as his fingers gripped and spread the actor's ass cheeks. Raising his head, Mike spit down into the tight, circular opening and then used a finger to work the saliva up into the dark confines of Steven's rectum.

"Oh, God," Steven gasped and let his head fall back on the mat. "Get that finger up inside me. Yeah, that's it."

Mike began to finger fuck Steven, spitting now and then to keep the opening lubricated. After loosening his hole with one finger, Mike added a second and, a short time after that, a third. He pushed three fingers deep into Steven's ass, his lips parted as he watched the reddening muscle spread around his knuckles and allow them access. Steven continued to lick and suck at Mike's asshole and grunted encouragement as his partner penetrated him with his fingers.

The director continued to call out direction to the men, moving around them just out of camera range to look at the action from all angles. He was heavy, out of shape, and sweat glistened on his pale forehead as he flounced about beneath the hot sun, his arms flapping and his face squeezing tight in concentration. He had yet to notice Charlie's presence at the side of the pool.

As Charlie watched the men writhing before him, his cock began to throb. The sun was hot out in the open and he peeled off his flannel shirt, exposing his broad, tanned, hairy chest. Work on the farm and a weight set in his parents' basement had helped him build up his physique. He kept his eyes on the actors by the pool and reached down to massage his expanding cock.

"You the fluffer?" a deep voice asked and Charlie jumped. He had been so absorbed in the couple being filmed he had failed to notice the man sitting in a chaise to his left. The sun was behind the man and spiked directly into Charlie's eyes.

"Uh, yeah," Charlie stammered, squinting in the glare. "Are you a member of the crew?" He stepped forward and shaded his eyes.

"In a manner of speaking," the man replied. "I'm Rock Harding."

"Oh, nice to meet you." Charlie looked the nude man over in awe. He was built like a ton of bricks. Every muscle in his body was crisply defined beneath a smooth layer of tanned skin. A thin coating of dark hair covered his body, thicker on his forearms. His cock lay soft between his legs, resting on the cushion formed by his shaved, pendulous balls. He had a square jaw with a shallow cleft in his chin, two days of stubble, dark, close cropped hair and deep brown eyes that pinned Charlie to the spot. "Oh," Charlie breathed at the sight of him. "Are you an actor?"

"No. I'm a porn star." Rock said and spread his legs, resting a foot to either side of the chaise. "I would like to be up and fully aroused in about five minutes. Think you can do that?"

"I can try," Charlie mumbled and fell to his knees alongside the gorgeous hunk of man before him. He slurped up Rock's stocky prick and began to suck, reaching down and wrapping his fingers around the magnificent set of balls.

"Oh, that's it," Rock whispered and tipped his head back. Charlie felt the member in his mouth begin to lengthen and increased the suction, feeling his throat muscles tighten up as he tugged a little more forcefully on Rock's sack.

16

Running his tongue along the shaft, Charlie moved his oral attention down to Rock's balls and watched with interest as the saliva slick dick continued to expand. How big was this guy? He ran his tongue along the smooth balls, sucking up one then the other and darting his tongue down to the base of Rock's testicles.

"Oh yeah, that's nice," Rock groaned quietly. Off in the background, Charlie could hear the director still talking his actors through their scene. "Suck my cock again. Take it all the way to the root."

Charlie obediently lowered his mouth over the sturdy, tanned cock. Rock was big, probably nine inches at least, and Charlie had to fight back a gag as he pushed his nose down into the man's perfectly trimmed pubic hair.

"Oh, you fucker," Rock grunted. "Not very many people can take all of me." Rock's hips shifted up, pushing his cock even deeper into his throat, and Charlie felt the weight of Rock's big, hair flecked hand come down on the back of his head. He inhaled the smell of suntan lotion and sweat through his nose and worked his tongue along the shaft of Rock's impressive boner.

Fingers fumbled with the snap of Charlie's jeans and then pulled his zipper down and soon Rock was jacking Charlie off with a big, meaty fist. Charlie reached back and pushed his jeans down to his thighs and felt Rock's fingers wrap around his balls and the base of his cock. Charlie groaned around the girth of Rock's dick and eased his head up, starting to suck furiously at the massive member.

"Jesus, you got a big dick yourself," Rock said in a voice throaty with lust. The timbre of the man's voice sent goose bumps rising along Charlie's skin as he pumped his fist along the shaft of Rock's prick and fastened his mouth on the ballooning head.

Rock spit into his hand and then reached back down to grab Charlie's cock in a strong grip. He began jacking him quickly, pumping out a copious amount of pre cum to coat the head and upper shaft of Charlie's boner.

Charlie could feel himself getting closer to climax and began to suck and stroke Rock's dick faster. A few moments later Charlie felt Rock's dick swell and then suddenly his mouth was filled with the hot, sharp taste of the man's semen. It seemed to be never ending as the torrent of cum flooded his mouth and throat and spilled out over his lips. As he came, Rock let out a deep, guttural groan.

Raising his head, Charlie let the cum bubble out over his chin as his hand continued to pump the slowing vestiges of spunk from Rock's deflating dick. He leaned down to suck the softening cock as the actor's fist continued to bang along his prick. And then Charlie felt himself tumble over into the abyss of orgasm and grunted around Rock's prized prick. His load exploded out of his penis and splattered over the tanned, sweaty skin of Rock's hairy thighs.

"Oh yeah, fluffer man," Rock grunted. "Shoot that load on my legs. Oh, yeah. That's hot."

And then the screaming began.

"What are you doing?!" a high pitched voice shrieked in his ear. "What the *fuck* are you doing?"

Charlie sat back, more cum burbling out of his mouth, and looked up into the bright red face of the large, sweaty director. "Huh?"

"I asked you a fucking question!" The man leaned down and wiped some of the cum off Charlie's chin. "What the fuck is this? Huh?"

Charlie blinked at the spunk dripping off the man's fingers. "It's, um, cum, sir."

"No shit," the man snapped. "And why did you feel you were entitled to come here to my set and suck off my lover? Huh? Any reason for that?"

"Your ... your lover?" Charlie looked over at Rock who was watching the director through half-lidded eyes, a smirk on his face. Charlie looked back at the man before him. "I'm sorry. I didn't know he was your – I thought he was next up and was my customer. I just thought he needed to be hard for the next scene and I . . ." Charlie's voice faded out.

The director straightened up and glared at Rock. "Typical." He then directed his attention back to Charlie. "Get dressed and get out. Not only did you fluff the wrong man, you actually made him cum. Jesus! Don't come back until you learn what a fluffer is supposed to do. Tell Kinitia she owes me a free service."

He turned his back and Charlie scrambled to his feet, pulling up his jeans and wiping his face on his shirt as he fled through the house. He ran down the driveway and out to the road where he flagged down a passing taxi and cowered in the backseat as he headed back to the office. What was Kinitia going to do to him? Would he lose yet another job?

Charlie hung his head and fought back tears. What was he going to do?

He was never going to make it in this city.

2
The Wrath Of Kinitia

Charlie scurried through the blessedly empty reception area of the office, his shirttail hanging out and his eyes cast down. Kinitia was nowhere in sight. He breathed a sigh of relief and darted into the bathroom, closing and locking the door behind him. After washing his face and making himself presentable, he carefully eased the door open.

Kinitia Jones stood directly outside the door, her arms folded over her chest and her eyes narrowed. Her lips were pressed tightly together, so tight they had almost vanished.

Charlie nearly yelped at the sight of her. "Oh!"

"You fucked up, didn't you?" Kinitia said in an even voice.

"Y-yes," Charlie said. "I didn't know who he was, I mean, he looked like a porn star and he said he wanted to be hard . . ."

Kinitia held up a hand, palm out, and he stopped talking. She shook her head and started pacing the hall. "I told you specifically that this was my most difficult client. Cedric and I have a lot of history between us. And not only did you go down on his *lover*, you got the guy off!" She threw her hands in the air. "You do know the purpose of your job, don't you?" Charlie opened his mouth to reply but she rushed on, speaking fast. "You are supposed to arouse the men or keep the men aroused prior to them going before the cameras. Nothing more. You do not bring them to orgasm and you certainly don't bring yourself to climax. Do you understand that?" Charlie hesitated, not sure if he should respond. But Kinitia stopped and whirled on him, her eyes blazing and her extensions swirling around her face. "Do you?"

"Yes!" Charlie blurted. "I know what I'm supposed to do. I just . . . I got carried away. It was my first time and it was all so ... overwhelming." He sighed and lowered his eyes. "I'm sorry."

Kinitia straightened up and some of the anger seemed to seep away as she snapped quietly, "Well next time keep yourself rooted a little better, would you?"

Charlie blinked. "You're not firing me?"

She folded her arms and stood firm before him. "I should. But I give all my new hires one fuck up. You just happened to cash yours in on the very first day. Consider this a warning shot across your bow." She shook her head. "I should have gone with you on your first assignment, but we've been so busy around here." She squinted at him and said, "Please be more careful next time."

"I will. I'm sorry."

Kinitia shook her head again and narrowed her eyes. "You remind me of someone."

"Really?" Charlie said, slightly fortified by the possibility of getting on Kinitia's good side. "Who?"

"Doris."

His face fell. "Doris?"

"Yeah. Doris." Kinitia turned to head back to the desk and Charlie followed.

"Doris Day?" he asked, confused and slightly insulted.

Kinitia laughed. "Her too. But the other Doris was a girl who was trained by my grandmother."

"Trained?" Charlie said. "Trained in what?"

"Dance."

"Oh, like ballet?"

"No." Kinitia gave him a flat stare, watching his reaction. "She taught pole and lap dancing."

Charlie blinked. "As in strippers?"

Kinitia smiled. "There it is again, that look Doris used to get." She sat back and shook her head at the memories. "Doris stepped off the bus from Georgia and into my grandmother's club. She was stacked and had legs up to her chin, but that girl was as dumb as road kill sometimes."

"Hmm," Charlie said, trying to decide if the dumb comment applied to him. But Kinitia was remembering Doris and did not acknowledge him.

"Grammy took one look at Doris and hired her on the spot. No audition, nothing. Just big tits and stilts for legs." Kinitia laughed again. "And that girl could dance. She made a small fortune working for my grandmother and moved to Key West when she retired." Kinitia fell quiet, absorbed by her memories. "She made the best chocolate chip cookies I have ever tasted."

"So your grandmother owned the strip club?"

Kinitia gave him a smirk. "Does that shock you?"

Charlie blinked and shrugged. "No." Yes, actually, it did. "I've just never heard of a grandmother owning a strip club, that's all."

Kinitia laughed. "Yeah, I guess you don't see a lot of that in Idaho. Truth is, there isn't that much of it out here in LA either." She tipped her chair back. "My mother was a dancer in the club and got pregnant by the owner, some con man named Quentin Cossel. My grandmother tried to get her to quit but my mother was very strong willed, seventeen-years-old, and living on her own and she just kept right on dancing. So my grandmother gathered the savings my grandfather had left her when he passed on, took out a small business loan and bought the club from Quentin."

"Who happened to be your father, right?" Charlie said, trying to keep the players straight.

"Right." Kinitia nodded. "Grandma sent Quentin packing and let my mother keep dancing until her seventh month. She cleaned the place up and hired girls who were down on their luck, got them off drugs and helped them get back on their feet."

"Jeez, she sounds like she was a real strong person."

"Oh, she still is," Kinitia replied. "She lives in a condo group down in San Diego off the money she made from the club. She ran that place with a stern hand and a firm heart, and she wasn't afraid to jump in and do any job. She'd tend bar, wait tables, work the door, clean up; she did everything in that place. And after I was born she pretty much raised me."

"Is that how you got into this business?" Charlie asked.

Kinitia nodded. "In a way. I met some people through working at the bar. Grandma gave me a lot of good business advice, whether I wanted it or not."

"What's your grandmother's name?"

"Tinitia Jones."

"You were named after her."

"Yep." The phone rang and Kinitia glanced at the instrument then looked back up at Charlie, the soft look gone and replaced by a more stern, all business expression. "Go home and get some sleep, Farm Boy. Come in tomorrow at eight a.m. We're going to have a busy day."

She answered the phone and Charlie breathed a sigh of relief. He had dodged a bullet and kept his job. He might be able to afford to live in LA after all. He left the office and caught the bus home. When he approached the door to his building, Ken Carlton, the senior member of Fluffers, Inc., appeared from the shadows.

"Hi Charlie," Ken said. His hands were in his pockets and he shuffled his feet. "Heard you had a bad day."

"You could say that," Charlie grumbled. He unlocked the door and led Ken up to his small studio apartment. "What are you doing here?"

"Thought you might like some company. Maybe we could go out or something." Ken sat on the futon that doubled as Charlie's bed.

"Sounds good. I could use a distracting evening out." Charlie took a quick shower then wrapped the towel around his waist and entered the main room of his apartment. Ken was stretched out on the futon, nude and sporting a boner.

"Maybe we could start here and work our way to the street?" Ken asked with a grin.

Charlie smiled. He dropped the towel on the floor and moved forward. Leaning down, he kissed the tip of Ken's cock, then ran his tongue along its length. Ken sighed with pleasure and reached out to grab Charlie's quickly stiffening dick.

Taking Ken's balls in his hand, Charlie massaged them with his tongue, layering them with saliva and sucking gently on each one.

Lifting the heavy sack of loose skin, Charlie fastened his lips on the tender spot at the base of Ken's testicles and sucked longingly.

"Oh, man," Ken groaned. "That's nice. Yeah, keep that up."

Charlie kissed and sucked and licked the skin of Ken's perineum, slowly working his way to the soft, wrinkled hole of his ass. A halo of light brown hair ringed the gasping muscle and Charlie ran his tongue through it, matting it down with spit as he lapped at Ken's anus.

"Yeah, eat my ass," Ken said. He raised his legs and grabbed the backs of his knees in his hands, giving Charlie more room to maneuver. Moving onto the futon, Charlie focused all his attention on the sensitive pucker of Ken's asshole, slipping his tongue up inside then running it firmly across the surface. He filled the dark, swampy hole with spit and worked a finger up inside Ken's body.

"Oh, that's right, get another one in there," Ken moaned. "Work that hole. Get them up in there."

Charlie slid a second finger up beside his first and started finger fucking Ken's ass. He leaned down and took the man's cock in his mouth, sucking in time with the rate of his fingers.

"Jesus, Charlie!" Ken reached down and lifted the younger man's face up off his cock. "You've got to slow down. This is really fucking hot and I could have cum in your mouth already, but you need to learn how to pace yourself."

Charlie kept his fingers moving slowly in and out of Ken's ass "Okay, Ken. Teach me."

"All right. First, suck gently and slowly. Long, slow strokes along the whole cock. When you start working the upper half and the head is when you're serious about getting a guy off." Ken watched Charlie start sucking his cock slowly and then let his head drop down onto the mattress. "Yeah, that's it. Keep it slow and deep. Oh, yeah. Good. Very good. You don't want me to cum, you just want me to be hard."

Charlie's fingers continued to fuck Ken's hole, working up high enough to rub against his prostate. Ken groaned again and shifted his hips to begin pumping up into Charlie's face. Charlie opened his throat and took the entire length of him, all eight inches, down to the soft bush of Ken's pubic hair. He could feel pre cum leaking from his own rigid cock and was amazed he had the stamina after having cum twice that day.

Ken reached down and lifted Charlie's head again, looking him in the eye. Charlie's lips were swollen and wet and Ken fought the urge to lean forward and kiss him.

"If a guy starts to fuck your face, you need to back off." Ken said. "He can't start moving his hips or he'll cum. Got it?"

Charlie nodded and licked his lips. "Got it."

"Okay." Ken looked at him for a minute, then said. "End of lesson. Get your dick up my ass and fuck the shit out of me."

Charlie smiled and moved to kneel between Ken's legs, raising them and resting the ankles on his shoulders. He rolled a lubed condom onto his wet, slick cock then pressed slowly, steadily into Ken's ass. He felt the tight embrace of Ken's rectal muscles and groaned, turning his head to kiss the sweaty calf next to his face.

"Oh, fuck!" Ken said. "You are thick. Uh!"

Charlie's balls swung up against the crack of Ken's ass and his pubic hair grazed the man's tightening balls. He stayed buried to root in Ken's ass for a minute, leaning forward to kiss him deeply before beginning to pump his hips. He started slowly, then built up speed until he was steadily battering Ken's ass with his full seven and a half inches.

"Tighten that fuckin' ass," Charlie grunted. "I want to feel your muscles clench down on my cock. Oh, yeah! That's it. Grab that cock, suck it with your ass." Charlie's hips burned his cock deep into Ken's hole, plowing between his hairy, sweaty ass cheeks.

"Fuck me, oh yeah!" Ken gasped. "Fuck that ass. Slam your cock into me. Uh! I'm cumming! Uh!"

Ken stroked himself to climax, his first shot hitting up over his head on the arm of the futon. The rest of his semen spattered over his chest and belly. He was bathed in sweat, gasping for breath and still riding Charlie's dick.

"Oh, that's so fuckin' hot," Charlie groaned. "You've got a tight ass. Oh yeah. Yeah, I'm going to cum. Uh! Uh!" He emptied his load into the condom embedded deep inside Ken's anal cavity.

Charlie fell onto Ken's body and got his breath back. He eased himself from the man's red, gaping hole and stripped off the condom. Walking to the bathroom he flushed it away and splashed water on his face.

"That was really hot," Ken said, still sprawled on the futon. "You've got some good moves, farm boy."

Charlie grinned and handed him a beer. "Thanks, you're pretty hot yourself. How come you haven't been in any movies?"

"Who said I wasn't?" Ken asked, slightly insulted.

"Oh, sorry. I just assumed you wouldn't be a fluffer if . . . Sorry. I'm just a naïve idiot." Charlie fell back on the futon and tried to fight off the dark mood he could feel descending. Kinitia was right he was a Doris.

"Hey," Ken said. "I didn't mean to make you feel bad. I guess I'm real sensitive about it. I made about twenty movies a few years ago, but the guy I signed a contract with took me for every dollar I had earned. This business is full of piranha and goldfish, and I just happened to be a goldfish."

"What do you think I am?" Charlie asked.

"A goldfish . . . with teeth." Ken smiled. "Let's go get dinner."

The following morning, Charlie walked into Fluffers, Inc. with a new attitude. He could do this job. After dinner the night before, he had practiced on Ken some more. He had been able to keep him hard for over an hour without cumming. He thought back to when Rock had cum, it had covered Charlie's face and caused him to cum as well. Just the smell of semen could bring Charlie to orgasm. He loved the sharp odor and salty taste.

Kinitia was on the phone, arranging times for her team of fluffers for that day. She smiled at Charlie, the previous day's fuck up seemingly forgotten. Charlie's spirits soared even higher at the touch of her smile and he headed to the waiting area where he grabbed an apple and sat down to watch *Beaches* with the other employees.

Shortly after his arrival, Charlie was on his way to an outdoor set somewhere in a national park. Kinitia had loaned him her car for the trip and he had nervously taken the keys from her exquisite ebony fingers. He wondered how the director had convinced the ranger to let him film in the area. Probably promised a good oral workout from some of the actors.

26

Charlie checked the directions as he followed a winding road up into the wooded hills and soon came to a small, abandoned cabin built next to a waterfall. The scenery was gorgeous. Who knew this kind of world existed just outside of LA?

He approached the cabin, hearing voices from within as he got closer. He ran his fingers through his hair and carefully opened the door to the cabin, stepping inside and blinking into the lights of a camera.

"Cut!" a voice shouted. "Who the fuck is that?"

"I'm from Fluffers, Inc.," Charlie said and raised his hand to block the light. "I'm sorry, did I interrupt something?"

"Just a fucking scene," the unseen voice shouted again. "Get out of the fucking picture!" Charlie started to retreat back through the door but stopped as the voice shouted at him again. "Not that way! You've already ruined it. Get in here and stay out of the way! I'll send him over to you when I need you. Until then shut up and stay out of sight."

Charlie walked through the brightly lit room, his upper lip sweating from nerves and the temperature in the cabin. The lights were so hot! He found an old straight-backed chair off in a corner and sat down. The legs wobbled beneath him and he carefully shifted position until he found what felt like a semi-stable spot on the chair.

Looking around, he saw two actors seated on a couch placed in front of the door he had just entered, one white and the other black. They were fully dressed and rehearsing lines, talking to each other in measured tones. He took a few deep breaths and calmed himself down.

The director was young and handsome with dark, wavy hair and a thick mustache. He was wearing shorts and a tank top, exposing a thick mat of chest hair. The cameraman beside him was chewing gum with a bored expression as he watched the two men on the couch.

The filming began and Charlie watched with interest as the scene progressed. The men quickly got naked and began to kiss and fondle each other. Soon they were sprawled over the couch in a 69 position, their large cocks glittering in the light of the camera as the director coached them through some of the actions.

"Dirk, take his cock deeper than that, open your throat and let him fuck your face," the director said to the white actor who was on the bottom. "That's it. Good."

The actor on top placed his knees on the arm of the couch over Dirk's head and began to pump his hips, dropping his cock down into Dirk's throat and pulling out again. Dirk kept his mouth open as his partner descended over him, then tightened his lips around the man's dark skinned shaft as he pulled out. The difference between the top actor's black dick and Dirk's tanned face made a good contrast in the bright lights of the camera.

"Good, Harris," the director said. "Get your cock deep in his throat. Fuck his face and keep sucking his cock. Dirk, pull Harris' balls out from between his legs, I want a shot of those beauties."

Harris, the black actor, began to pump his hips deeper, dipping his cock to the hilt into Dirk's mouth. Dirk reached up and grabbed the loose skin of Harris' sack then pulled it out from between his legs. Harris groaned at the sensation as he sucked Dirk's dick.

"Good, good," the director coached. "Nice, long strokes. Keep showing me good length. In and out, in and out. Get me hard. Good. Now let's see some rimming. Get your tongues in those holes, get 'em wet."

At the director's command, the actors moved back to work on one another's assholes. Their tongues caressed and penetrated closely shaved and sweat shrouded sphincters. Harris' big, loose balls lay spread across Dirk's chin and the actor on top pumped his hips slightly to rub his sensitive hole over Dirk's five o'clock shadow.

Charlie watched the men on the couch, his eyes wide and his cock at full mast. The actors were, of course, incredibly handsome and, as usual, well endowed. Their obvious enjoyment of having sex felt contagious. His head was almost spinning with unreleased testosterone. Why had he waited so long to move to California?

"Hi there," a deep voice whispered in his ear and Charlie jumped. Turning he found himself eye to eye with Rock Harding, the actor he had made cum the day before. The man was crouched next to his chair, his dark eyes soft and gentle.

"Oh, hi," Charlie whispered back with an edge. "Thanks for getting me in trouble yesterday."

"Yeah, sorry about that. You just looked really sexy when you took off your shirt." Rock offered his hand. "No hard feelings?"

Charlie smirked and blushed as he shook with the man. "Nice pun."

Rock grinned. "Thanks." They watched the scene in silence together. Harris had shifted position and was kneeling on the couch with Dirk pressed up against the arm. Harris held Dirk's hips up in the air as he sucked the man's cock and ran his pink tongue down over his balls to his glistening asshole. Curling his tongue tight, Harris prodded Dirk's twitching hole as his partner groaned and grunted and encouraged him deeper. Dirk reached up and grabbed his own feet, pulling them back and raising his ass so Harris could get at it more readily.

Harris sat back, his thick, hard cock standing straight out from his pubic hair, and slid a finger deep into Dirk's ass. Dirk closed his eyes and moaned as Harris began to slowly finger fuck him. Leaning forward, Harris let several wads of spit fall onto the reddened muscle and used his finger to work them up into Dirk's body. After a few more strokes, Harris added a second and then a third finger as Dirk groaned and squirmed beneath his attentions.

The director yelled, "Cut!" and Rock stood up as Charlie shifted position. He tried to keep from looking at Rock's bulging crotch that was suddenly right at his eye level. What was Rock doing here?

"Okay, we're going to start the fuck sequence," the director said and turned to look at Charlie. "Get Rock ready to go. He's up in fifteen minutes."

Charlie's eyes went wide and he looked up at the gorgeous hunk of man beside him. Rock grinned and winked down at him as he unbuttoned his shirt.

"You're in this movie?" Charlie whispered.

"Yeah. Surprised?" He peeled his shirt off and flexed his muscles. "And this time it's for real."

"Are you sure?" Charlie cursed his luck and shook his head. What if Rock's director boyfriend found out about this? What would happen then? Rock was Cedric's lover. Cedric would probably stick Charlie's head on a stake in front of the offices of Fluffers, Inc. to serve as a warning.

Before Charlie could get too panicked about the situation, Rock was standing nude beside him and pulling slowly on his thick, tanned penis.

"Shall we?" Rock said with a smile. He turned his hips and leaned in close.

Charlie took a breath then opened his mouth and sucked the man in. He buried his nose in the soft hair surrounding his groin and breathed in Rock's scent. He smelled of sweat and the slight tang of citrus, as if he had spread orange peels on his body. Fighting back a groan, Charlie worked his mouth along the steadily lengthening pole. His hands wrapped around Rock's low hanging balls and pulled them even lower, twisting and stroking the freshly shaved surfaces.

"Oh, that's nice," Rock whispered. He closed his eyes and ground his hips so his cock made circular motions in Charlie's mouth.

Remembering Ken's warning from the night before, Charlie backed off and ran his tongue along the shaft. He could feel blood pumping into the thick tube of flesh through the blue vein that stretched along its length. Unable to help himself, Charlie reached up and ran his hand over the muscular stomach above him. The hair on Rock's torso parted between his fingers as the dick alongside his cheek reached full erection. Charlie opened up and took him in again, the head tickling the back of his throat. He could taste the pre cum starting to leak from the slit.

"Oh, that's so nice," Rock whispered. He spread his legs and bent his knees, a light sheen of sweat breaking out on his body. "Get a finger up inside my hole."

Charlie moved his fingers back further and felt the man's hard gluts part as Rock reached back and spread his ass cheeks. The soft, puckered muscle gasped opened and admitted Charlie's index finger. He slid it up inside the gorgeous man before him and felt the sphincter tighten around his knuckle.

With a loud snap, the chair beneath Charlie suddenly gave way and he found himself falling. As he hit the floor, Charlie's jaw snapped up and Rock let out a howl of pain as Charlie's teeth bit down into his cock. At the same time, his finger rubbed roughly up against Rock's prostate. The combined bite and poke at his prostate was just enough pain to push the porn star over the edge. His dick erupted, spilling his carefully built up load into Charlie's mouth. The cum washed out over Charlie's lips and down his chin.

"What the fuck is going on?" the director screamed.

Rock pulled his injured dick from between Charlie's lips, cum still shooting up onto Charlie's face. The smell and taste of Rock's load took Charlie over the edge and he came in his jeans without touching himself. That had never happened to him before. What was it about Rock Harding that made him so crazy?

"Oh fuck!" Rock groaned, holding his aching cock. "He bit me!"

The director stood over Charlie, his eyes cold. "You bit him?"

"I couldn't help it," Charlie said, spraying cum as he spoke. "The chair broke."

"Jesus," the director hissed. Turning to Rock, he took the injured member in his hand and looked it over. "He didn't break the skin at least."

"It's pretty sore, Rod," Rock said quietly.

Rod looked up at him, annoyed and concerned. "Too sore to shoot a scene?"

Rock glanced down at the terrified look on Charlie's face. "I guess not. But I'll need some time to get my load back."

Rod shook his head and turned to look around the broiling room. "Chris!" A man holding a boom mike jumped up and ran over. "Get Rock hard again and keep him up for at least an hour. Be careful, his dick was injured in a slip and fall." The director glared at Charlie as he said the last part and then crossed the room to continue filming. Over his shoulder he said, "You can leave, fluffer. And tell Kinitia not to even *think* about billing me for this session."

"Wait a minute," Rock said in a commanding voice. Rod stopped and looked at him. "Let the fluffer do his job. It wasn't his fault the chair broke."

Rod opened his mouth to say something, then snapped it shut. Looking at Charlie, he asked, "Think you can do it without making him cum again?"

Charlie nodded and reached up to wipe off his chin.

"All right," the director said. "But this is your last chance."

Charlie got up and looked at Rock. "Thanks."

Rock smiled. "No problem. Let's go out by the water."

Charlie followed Rock out a back door and they both cleaned up in the crystal clear, cold water. Charlie dried his face with his shirt and looked up at the bronze god before him. "Sorry I bit you."

Rock shrugged. "It wasn't your fault. Just be careful this time. Sit on the ground or something."

Charlie laughed. "Okay. I'll be careful."

"Think you can handle having my dick in your mouth for an hour?" Rock asked, his mouth turning up in a sexy, flirtatious grin.

"I can try," Charlie replied and grinned back. Suddenly he felt like a piranha.

"Let's get to it then," the actor said and sat on the warm, flat surface of a rock by the waterfall.

Charlie took a breath and moved forward to kneel between Rock's thighs.

3

Rock Steady

Charlie knelt between Rock Harding's strong, hairy legs and began to gently suck the man's penis. He gingerly pressed his hands around the base of the organ, careful not to touch the bruised portion where he had bitten into the delicate skin.

"That feels really nice," Rock said. A massive hand rested gently on the back of Charlie's head. "You've got a very talented mouth and tongue."

Charlie accepted the compliment in silence, focusing all his attention on getting the man fully aroused and keeping him there. Releasing the slowly thickening flesh, Charlie began to stroke it carefully as he moved his mouth down to Rock's magnificent set of balls. He lathered them with spit, running his tongue over the loose tan skin and tasting the salty vestiges of Rock's last orgasm.

The taste of the dried semen set his cock to twitching and soon Charlie's own dick was hard. It strained against the semen-starched fabric of his underwear, wanting desperately to be freed. But Charlie kept his hands away from himself and continued to lick, suck, and tongue Rock's equipment.

"You know, I really like to have my ass eaten out," Rock stated and before Charlie knew what was happening, the man had stood up and turned his back on the fluffer. Bending over, Rock reached back and spread his muscular ass cheeks, exposing his glorious shaved hole. It was so beautiful Charlie could only sit and gaze at it in awe for a moment. The skin all around Rock's asshole was tanned, a testament to his sunbathing ritual. Hair lightly covered the cheeks of his ass, but the crack and skin around the pink, puckered opening were hairless.

Charlie moved in and gently licked around the wrinkled tissue of Rock's anus. His tongue tentatively flickered in and out of the pulsing muscle, tasting the essence of the man before him. Reaching up between Rock's legs, Charlie took hold of his pulsing cock and softly stroked it, careful not to excite him too much and make him cum yet again. He couldn't afford to be responsible for Rock's orgasm a third time!

"Oh, that's it," Rock whispered. "Work that tongue up inside my ass."

Charlie probed deeper with his talented tongue, teasing and licking and sucking at the big man's sensitive opening. The sphincter throbbed beneath his lips as Charlie planted a deep, prodding kiss at the entrance to Rock's hot, wet tunnel. How he longed to slip his cock up inside this man, pound into him until they both came in a frenzy of passion.

Charlie checked his fantasy and moved back, keeping only his tongue at the slick hole. He licked up and down the crack of Rock's ass then moved back to his balls, sucking them gently. He could feel pre cum forming in the slit of Rock's cock and knew he was achieving his goal. The man's balls were churning up a good load of cum for his next scene.

Sooner than expected, Rock was called back inside the cabin. As he walked off, he lay a large warm palm against Charlie's cheek. "Thanks for the workout, fluffer."

"Charlie."

Rock grinned. "Thanks, Charlie."

Rock's place was taken by Dirk, one of the actors from the previous scene. Dirk was handsome, but Rock outshone him easily. Dirk sat on the rock before Charlie and sneered at him. "Suck away, fluffer. I'm in another scene after this one."

Charlie lowered his face to the man's crotch and began to suck his soft cock. As the actor's dick hardened in his mouth, Charlie could not help but think about Rock Harding and the smell and taste of his body.

A few hours and several dicks later, Charlie's throat and jaw muscles were aching. He sat on the ground beneath a tree and watched the director instruct the actors contorting on the ground before him. They were filming beside the waterfall and three men were servicing Rock who lay on his back. Two were taking turns sucking and licking his dick while the third was busy stuffing his bulging cock down Rock's throat.

Charlie had been hard for almost two hours with no release and he was getting close to the end of his endurance. He was going to need to cum soon. Watching Rock deep throat the actor straddling his head was turning him on even more. Oh, how he longed to be fucking Rock's beautiful face. He could practically feel the muscles in Rock's chest tighten and release beneath his hands as his cock burrowed deep into the man's throat.

The men shifted position and Rock was on hands and knees, sucking Harris' dick while an actor lay sucking Rock's dick and Dirk began a sloppy, intense rim job. He licked and sucked at Rock's asshole, then slid three fingers deep into Rock's body cavity and reached down to pull roughly on his heavy balls, kissing the small of Rock's back and running his tongue along his vertebrae.

Charlie groaned quietly and sat on his hands to keep from touching himself.

A condom was produced and Dirk put it on and slid his cock deep into Rock's ass. Rock's expression tightened and he closed his eyes, his lips still fastened around Harris' black, glistening prick. Dirk began to pump into Rock's ass slowly then ground his hips in a circular motion. Rock moaned at the right times, pressing his hips back into the man to get the dick further up his ass as he continued to suck Harris and the man lying beneath him sucked Rock's prick.

The actor beneath Rock slid out and positioned himself behind Harris as Rock continued to suck the actor's cock. He rolled a condom onto his dick and then moved closer until he was kneeling between Harris' legs, his cock wedged between the actor's dark ass cheeks. After checking his aim, the actor sank slowly into Harris' hole, his pale dick vanishing as he penetrated the man completely. Harris groaned and closed his eyes, leaning his head back to kiss the actor fucking him as Rock kept up a steady rhythm of suction and Dirk continued to pound into Rock's asshole.

"Good!" Rod said. "Good! Keep going! We've got three cameras on you. Don't stop. Take it all the way to the cum shots. Pull out further on your backstrokes, Dirk. Good."

Harris let out a grunt and pulled his dick from between Rock's swollen lips. He ran his hand along the length for a moment then his expression tightened and the head of his cock pulsed as he shot a thick wad of cum up into Rock's face. The semen splashed over the actor's closed eyes and lips as Harris grunted and the actor behind him moaned as Harris' rectum tightened with his orgasm.

"Yeah!" Dirk said as another shot from Harris landed on the back of Rock's shoulder. "Cum on his face. Shoot your load. Oh, I'm cumming." Dirk pulled out of Rock's hole and stripped the condom off, firing his load onto the tanned, sweaty skin of Rock's lower back and ass cheeks. When he was done, Dirk smeared the puddles of cum around with the head of his dick.

Rock straightened up to lean back against Dirk's chest and the actor fucking Harris pushed him down then began driving harder and deeper into his asshole. Harris rode the actor's cock with eyes closed then moved forward and took Rock's hard, throbbing dick in his mouth and began to stroke and suck him with fast, sure motions. The actor behind him continued to pump into Harris' ass then pulled out and peeled the condom from his long, thick cock and jerked himself to an impressive orgasm. The thick, white semen spattered across Harris' dark skin and the actor gasped with each shot.

"Oh, yeah," Rock grunted, his eyes locked on the thinning puddles of cum across Harris' back and ass cheeks. He tipped his head back and kissed Dirk deeply while Harris continued to suck and stroke his dick. Raising his head, he said, "I'm cumming, oh yeah!"

Harris pulled Rock's dick from his mouth and closed his eyes. A massive blast of semen erupted from the bulging head of Rock's prick and arced up over Harris' shoulder to land on his back.

A second shot, just as impressive, coated Harris' face while the remainder spurted out onto the grass.

Charlie felt a tiny flame of pride burn in his chest at the amount and height of Rock's cum shot. Rod yelled, "Cut! Excellent!" and towels were tossed out to the actors. Pandemonium broke out as crewmembers began to run around striking the set.

Charlie left amidst the confusion of the disassembly of the cameras and stowing of the lights. He got Rod to sign the time card Kinitia had given him and then headed to the car. Glancing around, he tried to catch one last glimpse of Rock, but the man was nowhere to be found. He had probably already left.

The drive back into the city took three times as long because of traffic. Charlie sat and ran the day's events over in his mind, his cock maintaining a steady rigidity that begged for release. Finally unable to take it any longer, Charlie cut over and exited the highway. He drove along some surface streets until he came upon just what he needed: a gas station.

He parked in a side lot and entered a dimly lit restroom heavily scented with air freshener. Two stalls stood in the far corner and he took the one next to the wall, closing the door and dropping his jeans to sit on the commode.

Just as he was beginning to stroke himself, the door squealed open and a flood of light and city sounds rushed in. The door slammed shut and Charlie held his breath as he listened to the slow tread of the new arrival. The man eased open the door to the stall beside his and locked it behind him.

Turning his head, Charlie saw a hole cut in the stall wall just above the toilet paper dispenser. He had been so focused on jerking off he had failed to notice this interesting feature. Leaning forward, he peered through the hole and watched as the man next to him opened his jeans and pulled out a long, uncut cock.

Charlie licked his lips. He had sucked uncut cocks back home in the barn and enjoyed the way the foreskin hid the bulbous head beneath. It was like unwrapping a chewy, cream filled piece of candy.

The man stroked his fat prick and shook it a few times. The cock began to grow and Charlie could not take his eyes off it.

What a beautiful penis! He started to stroke himself again, pre cum pumping out of his dick with each pass of his hand. He was so close to orgasm it hurt.

The man beside him shifted position and slipped the beautiful, uncut cock through the hole in the wall. It hung invitingly before Charlie, a single pearl of pre cum gathering at the slit.

His lips parted just enough and Charlie leaned in to take the man down his throat. His jaw ached and his throat threatened to shut down, but he could not resist this fine piece of meat. Releasing his grip on his own raging hard-on, Charlie began working the thick cock before him with his hand and mouth. A groan sounded softly from the opposite side of the wall, causing Charlie to echo the sentiment around his mouthful of meat.

The dick was quickly at full attention and Charlie pulled back the foreskin to reveal the wide, bulb-shaped head. He licked around the soft ridge where it met the shaft and then released the foreskin once again. Sheathing his teeth with his lips, Charlie grabbed the edges of skin and pulled it out away from the cock. The man moaned again.

Taking the foreskin in his fingers, Charlie continued to pull it up over the head and spread it open, allowing his tongue to slip inside. He licked all around the slick velvet head beneath, the taste of pre cum coating his throat. After several minutes of stretching the foreskin, Charlie released it and once more peeled it back away from the head.

Pre cum drizzled down the length of his cock as he sucked on the dick through the wall. His balls were aching with the urge to release, but he held back. He wanted this to be just right.

The uncut cock slowly withdrew and was replaced by a wrapped condom. Charlie took the package and quickly rolled the protection down over his oozing hard-on. He looked up and found an eager, pink asshole pressed up against the other side of the glory hole. Sticking his tongue through the wall, he teased the twitching hole and then moved back a little to spit into it. He used his fingers to smear the saliva around and push it up into the dark recesses of the man's ass before standing up. His prick stood out from his groin ramrod straight, filled to its limit with blood.

Positioning himself, Charlie butted the blunt head of his cock up against the anxious hole of his receiving partner. With a steady pressure, he slid into the hot depths of the man's ass, burying himself as far as possible with the first thrust.

"Oh, yeah," the man grunted through the wall. "Fuck my ass."

"Yeah, you like that big cock up your ass, don't you?" Charlie said quietly. He gripped the top of the stall and started to pump his hips, watching as his dick moved in and out of the hole in the wall. The man's ass clenched around his cock and Charlie groaned. "Oh, tighten that ass. Bite down on my cock."

"Harder," the man moaned and Charlie began moving his hips faster, slamming into the mysterious asshole.

Before long, Charlie felt the familiar tingling in his dick and his balls pulled up, ready to eject their seed. He gasped and plunged into the man as his hips bucked and took him over the edge. His cock swelled where it lay tight up inside the man's rectum and cum filled the tip of the condom.

"Oh, fuck," Charlie gasped. "Oh, man." He pulled slowly out of the man's slick hole and peeled the condom off, dropping it in the toilet before sitting down again.

The man in the next stall turned back and began to stroke himself, bringing himself to climax and pushing his cock through the glory hole just before his first shot blew free. Charlie caught the cum in his mouth and sucked the remainder of the man's load out of his pumping cock. When he was spent, the man pulled his cock back through the wall, buttoned up his jeans, and walked out the door. Charlie never got a look at his face.

After cleaning himself up, Charlie returned to the car and found his way back to the highway. He felt drowsy from his orgasm and was looking forward to a relaxing night in front of the TV.

When he entered the office, Charlie heard voices coming from the waiting room down the hall. He walked into the room and found Kinitia and Ken sitting on one of the sofas, their heads bent together in serious conversation.

"He can't possibly do it, you know," Ken said soothingly.

"If anyone can figure out a way, it's him. Trust me, I've known him a long time. I just don't understand why he still has it in for me after all these years." Kinitia looked up and blinked in surprise. "Oh, hi Charlie. How did everything go this time?"

Charlie put the memory of biting down on Rock's dick out of his mind and smiled. "Fine. Here's the time card signed by the director. And, here are your keys." He handed the items over. "Is everything okay?"

Kinitia shrugged. "As okay as it ever is. That bitch Cedric is trying to put me out of business."

Charlie blanched. "Because of me?"

Kinitia shook her head. "No. Cedric and I have been shadow boxing with each other for a long time now. I don't understand why he's so fixated on tormenting me."

Ken shrugged. "He's just a vindictive asshole. There's nothing to understand." He turned to Charlie. "He's part owner of Tongue In Cheeks, another fluffer service, and is pissed off because the studio he does most of his work for has an exclusive contract to use Kinitia's fluffers. That plus only six of his employees have gone on to become stars and more than two dozen of her fluffers have gone into the business."

"Wow, two dozen?" Charlie said in amazement. "That's really something."

"Not when you see what happens to them after they get into the business," she said quietly. "I still feel responsible for them." She sighed and shook her head. "How did Grammy do it for so long?"

"Everyone makes their own choices, Kinitia." Ken stood up. "You going to be okay?"

She nodded up at him. "Yeah. Thanks for listening. I'll see you guys tomorrow."

Charlie followed Ken out of the office and down to the street where they parted company. Charlie caught the bus back to his apartment but found he was pacing the floor like a caged beast. He needed to get out and do something. The day's events had left him edgy and restless.

Packing a bag, he headed for the gym. Handsome men were in abundance, their tanned flesh sleek and tight over corded muscle. Everywhere he turned Charlie found movie star quality smiles, square jaws, and interested looks.

He climbed up on a Stairmaster in the back row and started his workout. In front of him a dozen Lycra covered asses bunched and released in time to the routines. Back in Idaho he could have never imagined such a sight: all those tight, pumping asses just begging to be worked over.

He worked out for just over an hour then hit the showers. He liked the layout of the gym because the changing room had individual showers, each with an opaque shower curtain to provide a semblance of privacy. As he washed away his sweat, Charlie glanced through a part in his curtain. In the shower directly across from his he could see through a gap in the far curtain where a well-built and well-endowed gym bunny stood under the spray. The man had soaped up his hairy, muscular chest and was working up lather around his groin when he raised his eyes and caught Charlie watching him. The gym bunny grinned and began to stroke his cock. The lather expanded and his dick quickly firmed up until it was standing straight out from his body. He was about seven inches long and cut, thicker at the base than the head. His balls had pulled up from the breeze through the part in the curtain and Charlie watched with interest as the man continued to stroke himself.

Feeling his own cock respond to the show, Charlie reached down and began to reflect the man's motions. He stroked slowly, bringing himself to full mast within a minute.

With a flick of his wrist, the gym bunny shut off the water to his shower and stepped across the hall to slip into the stall beside Charlie. He raised a finger to rest it against Charlie's lips and whispered, "Keep quiet and we won't get caught."

Charlie's stomach spun with excitement and he nodded. The man leaned forward and kissed him hard, his tongue barging past his lips and into Charlie's mouth where it fought with Charlie's tongue for dominance over the region. The gym bunny pressed his hard wet body tight against Charlie's own soapy skin and began to undulate. Charlie's cock was trapped between the two flat stomachs, being stroked by both sets of hard abdominal muscles.

Before he knew it, Charlie felt himself spun around and a finger probed deep into his asshole. He raised his left foot and rested it on a small ledge, giving the gym bunny more room to maneuver. The man slid another finger up inside his ass, then another, speeding up and then slowing down the finger fucking as the water sprayed over Charlie's back and the gym bunny's chest.

After working Charlie's hole for a few minutes, rubbing and stroking the sphincter and inner lining, the gym bunny pulled his fingers out and reached outside the shower curtain. He had brought his shaving kit with him when he had crossed the tile floor and now produced a condom from within its depths. He deftly rolled it onto his rock hard dick and lathered it up with soap.

"Ready?" the gym bunny whispered.

"Yeah," Charlie whispered back and winced as the man pushed into him. His sphincter widened to allow the foreign object passage but his rectal muscles were a little more reluctant to grant access. The gym bunny pulled back and pressed forward again, this time piercing Charlie with his entire length.

Placing his strong, tan hands on Charlie's shoulders, the gym bunny began to hump him with abandon. His hips pistoned back and forth like a well-oiled machine. The slap of his thighs and pelvis against Charlie's skin turned Charlie on even more. He could feel the man's balls swing up and knock against his own and Charlie reached down to grab both sets in his hand and tug on them.

"Oh, yeah," the gym bunny whispered. He ran his tongue around the curls of Charlie's ear and slipped the tip inside. Charlie groaned quietly and leaned back to kiss the man with his tongue hanging out.

The man's pace increased and then began to slow as he neared his climax. Charlie began to stroke himself, the pre cum washing away in the shower spray as his fist pummeled faster and faster along the reddening shaft.

"Uh, uh!" the man grunted, his hips banging more insistently against Charlie's ass cheeks as his prick fired its load into the condom.

Charlie straightened up, the gym bunny's cock clenched tight inside his ass, and focused his grip just beneath the ridge of the head of his cock. The gym bunny reached around and began tweaking his nipples as Charlie bent his knees and bucked his hips forward. Thick wads of cum spewed from the purple bulb of Charlie's dick and slid down the shower wall.

The gym bunny pulled out slowly and unrolled the condom from his cock. He leaned forward and kissed Charlie lightly on the mouth, rinsing off his dick in the process, then stepped out of the shower and disappeared toward the lockers.

Charlie washed up, lollygaging to allow the gym bunny time to get dressed and leave the changing room, thereby avoiding any awkward conversations. The encounter had been just that: an encounter, nothing more, and nothing less.

After drying off, Charlie got dressed and ran a brush through his hair. He wasn't very concerned with how he looked; he was just going to go home and hit the sheets. But when he stepped out from around the lockers, he ran full steam into a solid wall of spectacular pectorals.

"Oh, sorry," a deep voice mumbled and froze Charlie to the spot.

He raised his eyes and found himself looking up at the smiling face of Rock Harding. Charlie stepped back and blushed, suddenly wondering just how bad he looked.

"Hey, fluffer man," Rock said with genuine delight.

Charlie looked around in a panic. Had anyone heard him? "Careful how you say that. And it's Charlie."

Rock made a face and ducked his head, saying in a low voice, "Sorry. I forget sometimes. Done working out?"

Charlie shrugged and ran a self-conscious hand through his hair. "Yeah. I was a little restless tonight."

"Yeah, I know what you mean." The man rocked back on his heels and looked down at the floor. "Are you hungry?"

"Hungry?" Charlie repeated stupidly.

"Yeah, hungry," Rock explained. "Got to repair all the muscle tissue you broke down during your workout."

"Uh, well, um," Charlie stammered, stuck evenly between wanting desperately to go and terrified of what might happen if he did.

"Okay then, it's settled," Rock announced. "Wait for me in the lounge and I'll be right there."

Charlie nodded, trapped within the man's intense look. "Okay. I'll be in the lounge."

As he left the changing area, Charlie cursed himself and contemplated just leaving the gym. But, Rock was a client, albeit a sneaky, beautiful one, and it might be good for Kinitia's business and his own career to schmooze with a client. Then again, Rock was the lover of Kinitia's worst client from hell and, oddly enough, half owner in a competitor's company.

He sighed as he plopped himself down on a stool at the smoothie bar and ordered up a kiwi-strawberry-orange-banana shake. Who would have thought being a fluffer would ever become this complicated?

4

Clandestine

The line for the restaurant was long and Rock and Charlie had to wait in the bar. Charlie shifted uncomfortably on a stool, rubbing at a drop of smoothie on his sweatshirt as he eyed the crowd around him. He was wearing an old pair of sweats and worn, rather smelly workout shoes. He had taken no hair products along to the gym, expecting to simply head home and go right to bed after his workout.

Rock, in contrast, was dressed in a pair of well-fitted khakis and a gray cashmere pullover. His hair was perfectly coifed and his skin shone with a radiance that had every man and woman in the bar turning to gaze at him. The hundreds of eyes lingered on Rock's face and body, then shifted over to assess Charlie with looks of slight distaste or, worse, disbelief. They didn't seem to know what to make of the pairing on exhibit before them.

"Thanks for coming out with me tonight," Rock was saying as Charlie looked around.

"Huh?" He jerked his head back and looked up into Rock's deep brown eyes. "Oh, sure. No problem. A guy's gotta eat, right?"

They covered such meaningful topics as the weather, the current political brouhaha in Washington, and movies they wanted to see. Charlie found it amazing that earlier that day he had been sucking this man's cock and sliding his tongue up into his ass and now here he was, nervous as a Catholic schoolgirl at her first coed mixer.

The maitre d' approached Rock and whispered that his table was ready. Charlie was impressed. Most places he ate handed him a large plastic pager that flashed when he could be seated. They followed the tuxedo-clad man through the sea of other well-dressed diners to a corner booth. Charlie quickly slid into the half circle of the booth, eager to be sitting down and out of sight. Rock slid in along the other side of the velvet cushion and bumped a leg up against Charlie's knee, igniting a spark in his system that went straight to Charlie's crotch. He felt his cock twitch in response to this slight physical contact with the beautiful man beside him and fought back the swirl of fantasies that sprang unbidden to mind.

As he scanned the menu prices Charlie mentally checked his wallet to make sure he had brought a credit card with some space left on the limit. He could afford a dinner here if he did not eat anything but boxed macaroni and cheese for two weeks. That settled, Charlie contemplated his flurry of emotions surrounding Rock Harding as he pretended to read the menu. He had been orally servicing this man a few times and still it had not seemed as intimate as this dinner. When he had met Rock and provided fluffer service for him they had been surrounded by people and under the guise of work. And Charlie blamed himself for each incident in which he had made Rock cum, but in the dark recesses of his mind a small voice whispered that maybe, just maybe, Rock was so attracted to Charlie he couldn't contain himself.

"Escargot?"

Charlie blinked stupidly up at the waiter. "Huh?"

"Would monsieur like to sample an escargot?" The waiter tipped the plate a bit to display the dish.

"Um, okay." Charlie watched with wide eyes as the waiter placed two escargot onto his plate. He knew what they were, of course, just because he was from Idaho did not mean he was an uncultured dolt. He had seen *Pretty Woman* at least ten times and was now mentally reenacting Julia Roberts' escargot scene, sure he was going to embarrass himself. He carefully worked the meat from the shell and chewed on it thoughtfully. He had never had escargot before, and, based on this sample, he believed he did not ever want it again.

Just as Charlie was going to ask Rock something meaningful he had yet to come up with, the waiter was back. "Would you like to order now?"

Charlie smiled patiently and tried not to notice the waiter gazing at Rock with puppy dog eyes. The guy probably had all of Rock's tapes back at his apartment. The waiter took their order, accepted the menus, and walked away.

"Did you like the escargot?" Rock asked with a smile.

Charlie flashed a bright, false smile. "Sure."

They talked about work for a while, then Rock asked Charlie where he was from. When he heard the answer, Rock seemed very interested in life on a farm in Idaho and Charlie answered all of his questions with as much detail as possible. While he was talking he tried not to picture Rock bare chested, wearing jeans, boots and a Stetson while throwing hay in the barn.

Dinner was finished and the waiter was back with the bill. Giving Charlie a slightly sour look, he placed the small leather folder before Rock and scurried away. Charlie breathed a sigh of relief as Rock pulled out a credit card and then decided it was time to use the restroom. He gasped when he caught sight of his reflection in the mirror and clutched the counter before him. His hair was wildly disarrayed, his sweatshirt stained and torn in several places, and what looked like more smoothie stains marred the fabric of his sweat pants. He nearly collapsed in tears. How could this have happened?

He clawed at his hair, molding it into some semblance of order using spit and water, whimpering quietly as he worked. The door burst open and two men walked in laughing boisterously. Their laughter faded at the sight of Charlie and the men looked him over in amusement as they approached the urinals.

Charlie took a breath, ignoring the men peeing in the background, and looked himself square in the eye. He could get through this night. He was as good as anyone else in this restaurant. He squared his shoulders, set his jaw, and gave himself a quick nod. He could do this. Leaning down, he turned on the faucet to wash his hands one more time and promptly splashed water on the front of his pants.

Later that evening, Rock pulled up in front of the office of Fluffers, Inc. Charlie, eager to be free of this intoxicating, confusing, dangerously attractive man, immediately pushed open the door of the Navigator and jumped down to the street.

"Thanks for dinner," Charlie said, standing on his toes to peer over the seat.

Rock grinned. "You're welcome. Thanks for keeping me company. Sure you don't want me to wait and take you home?"

Charlie shook his head, thinking of the embarrassment he would suffer should Rock see the outside of his building, let alone the apartment contained within. "No thanks. There's a light on upstairs and I need to talk with Kinitia anyway."

"Okay. See you around."

Charlie watched the gigantic SUV pull away and let out a breath as his shoulders sagged. What a night! He was exhausted. He entered the building and tried the door to Fluffers, Inc. It was unlocked and a light was on in the back room.

Charlie warily approached the room and stopped just inside the door. On one of the couches, huddled up in a corner sat a man a few years younger than Charlie himself. He was hugging his legs to his chest and had pressed his forehead against his knees. He was crying softly, a sound that broke Charlie's heart. He had cried like this on several occasions back in Idaho, and no one had ever been around to comfort him.

"Hi there," Charlie said softly.

The man jerked his head up and swiped at his eyes, clearly embarrassed. "Oh, shit. I'm sorry. I didn't think anyone else was here."

"It's okay. I'm Charlie Heggensford. Are you new here?" He walked around the couch and sat beside the young man.

"Uh huh. I'm Billy Ransom."

Charlie smiled. "Great stage name. Are you an actor?"

Billy frowned at him. "It's not a stage name. I'm from Cleveland. I just started today."

"Oh. Sorry. I just started a few days ago." Charlie watched Billy wipe his eyes. "Why are you crying?"

"I'm no good at fluffing," Billy said tearfully. "I keep making them cum."

Charlie laughed. It was a deep, feel good laugh that released his tension of the evening and made him feel lighter than he had in weeks. "Oh, I'm so glad to hear you say that. I keep doing that too!"

"Really?" Billy asked with a smile.

"Really!" Charlie's eyes lit up. "We should practice. On each other."

Billy's smiled widened. "Okay. Who's first?"

"How about me?" a voice said from behind them and they both turned to find Ken Carlton leaning in the doorway.

"Ken, hi!" Charlie turned to Billy. "He's a really good teacher."

The three men were soon naked and sprawled out on the floor. Ken was leaning back against the sofa, his big eight-inch cock standing straight up as Charlie and Billy took turns swallowing it. They ran their tongues along his tight, pink shaft then Charlie lay on his back on the floor to scoot right up to Ken's balls, his nose pressed into the soft, damp flesh of the man's asshole. He breathed in the musk of Ken's ass and balls as he licked and slobbered the sensitive, shaved skin of his sack. Billy straddled Charlie's chest and moved his mouth slowly up and down along the hard, throbbing pole of Ken's cock.

"More slowly, Billy," Ken instructed gently. "You don't want me to cum yet."

"Oh, but I really do," Billy moaned. "I want you to cum all over my face and chest." He took a breath and swallowed Ken's dick until his nose was pressed into the man's pubic hair.

"Oh, fuck," Ken grunted. "You'll get your wish, you hot little fucker, but first you need to keep me hard for an hour."

Charlie reached down and smeared the slick puddle of pre cum that had collected at the tip of his dick over the head and upper shaft of his cock. His dinner with Rock had kept him hard nearly the entire time they had been in the restaurant and he had a massive load of cum built up and ready to go. He lapped at Ken's balls and sucked them into his mouth, tugging them gently away from his body. Ken groaned and pulled his knees up, giving Charlie room to move.

Billy released Ken's dick from his mouth, allowing it to slap against the hard, hairy ridges of Ken's stomach, and moved down to lick at the balls that Charlie was still sucking. His tongue slipped between Charlie's lips and caressed the tender orbs of Ken's balls where they lay in Charlie's mouth. Charlie and Ken both groaned under Billy's oral worship. Shifting his hips back, Billy felt Charlie's boner bump up against his balls and lifted his pelvis. His own hard, seven-inch prick lay up against Charlie's steadily leaking rod. Charlie wrapped his hand around both pulsating shafts of muscle and began to stroke them. Now it was Billy's turn to moan.

"That feels nice, Charlie," Billy breathed down into Charlie's mouth. He licked around Charlie's lips, then moved up to once more take Ken's cock into his mouth.

Charlie continued to stroke his and Billy's dicks, using a slow, steady rhythm. His pre cum dribbled out and slickened both cocks as well as his fingers. He tightened his grip a little more and picked up the pace of his strokes. With a final caress from his tongue, Charlie released Ken's balls and moved up to begin delicately probing the man's moist, velvety hole. He licked all around the twitching muscle of his anus, then slid his tongue up inside. Ken gasped and ground his hips down, forcing Charlie's tongue deeper into him.

"Oh, yeah, Charlie," Ken said through clenched teeth. "Get your tongue up my ass. Eat that ass out. Suck on it."

Charlie began sucking and licking at the hot, tender opening. His lips and tongue massaged and invaded the wrinkled sphincter, coating it with his saliva and stretching it open with his tongue.

Billy moved back to Ken's balls and began to suck them, picking up where Charlie left off. He reached up and slowly stroked Ken's dick, moving his fist the full length of the shaft and tightening his grip at the head.

"Goddamn, Billy," Ken whispered. "You've got a fuck of a nice touch there. I want to just fuckin' blow all over that pretty face of yours."

"Oh, man," Billy moaned around Ken's balls. "You're turning me on. I'm going to have to cum soon."

"Not yet," Ken instructed. "We hold our loads until the end, and we're not done yet."

Ken slowly got up and turned over so he was on all fours on the floor. Charlie adjusted his position and knelt behind Ken, spreading the man's firm cheeks and burying his face in the hairy furrow of his ass. Billy stretched out with his head beneath Ken's crotch and set to work sucking his dick, his own cock directly beneath Ken's face. Ken lowered his head and took Billy's blood gorged member into his mouth, sucking him slow and deep and working his tongue around the sensitive head and shaft.

Charlie moved down from Ken's spit drenched asshole and ran his tongue along the man's perineum. He picked up the low hanging set of balls in one hand and began to lick and suck at them, reaching up to slip a finger into Ken's anus as he worked his balls. Just beneath Charlie, Billy fought against his gag reflex as Ken's eight inches of hot, bloated meat filled his throat.

"Charlie, get the bowl of condoms from behind the bar," Ken said. "It's time to work on a different kind of lesson."

Charlie brought a large glass bowl filled with condoms to the sofa along with a bottle of lube. He wrapped his cock in latex and squeezed lube along the length. Ken lay on his back on the couch and hung his legs over the arm, lifting them with his hands behind his knees. Billy sat with his back against the couch and stretched his head back to lick at Ken's hole while Charlie positioned himself. He pressed slowly forward until his cock submerged itself completely into Ken's ass. The man groaned and closed his eyes as Charlie's cock filled him, the torpedo shape of it easily parting his rectal muscles.

As Charlie began to pump into Ken, Billy licked Charlie's balls, lapping at them each time they swung forward and slapped against his face.

"Billy," Charlie said without breaking stride. "Get a condom on that pretty dick of yours and jam it up my ass."

Billy leaped up and did as instructed. A moment later he was buried firmly between Charlie's ass cheeks as Charlie continued to fuck Ken. They found a matching rhythm and started to fuck each other faster and faster until the two hard cocks were pounding up into both hot assholes.

Charlie slowed his pace and pulled out of Ken's ass, allowing him to change position. Ken turned around and stood up, leaning forward over the arm of the couch. Charlie slipped back into him and started banging away, closing his eyes and ignoring the sweaty strands of hair that had fallen into his face.

Billy pulled out of Charlie and peeled off the condom. Stretching out along the couch, he opened his mouth and took Ken's dick in his mouth, reaching up to jerk the man off as he sucked on the large purple head. As he sucked furiously on Ken's dick, Billy worked his fist just as fast along his own cock.

"Oh, fuck!" Charlie moaned. "I'm going to cum, Ken."

"Pull out and shoot it on Billy," Ken grunted. He was right on the verge and knew he was going to blow soon as well.

Charlie reluctantly pulled his dick out of Ken's tight ass and stripped off the condom as he walked around the couch. Just as he reached the length of Billy's firmly muscled torso the first shot of cum fired up out of his cock and landed with an audible plop on the young man's smooth chest. Billy groaned around the length of cock in his throat and Charlie watched the speed of his fist pick up. Charlie fired load after load onto the man's torso and belly, aiming his spurting cock all along the length of the tan, muscular body stretched out beneath him. The semen landed on Billy's cock and added a light lubricant to his intense jacking.

"Oh, yeah," Ken said. "Here it comes, Billy."

Billy kept the fat, red cock in his mouth and let the thick, white fluid bubble up around his lips and down over the sides of his face and chin. In no time at all, Billy brought himself to orgasm and managed to land his first shot on Ken's thigh.

The three men caught their breath and then headed to the restroom to clean up. They giggled and pushed at each other, all three trying to use the sink at the same time. While they were in the restroom, they heard a soft sound from the front of the office that stopped them cold.

"What was that?" Charlie whispered, his eyes wide. They were naked and trapped in a tight, enclosed space.

"Sounds like someone's in the outer office," Ken said. "Keep quiet and I'll try to open the door." He flicked off the lights, plunging the room into claustrophobic darkness.

Charlie felt Billy press up against his back and reached around to place a reassuring hand on the man's thigh. They watched nervously as Ken eased the door open and leaned out into the hallway.

"Oh shit," Ken gasped quietly. He stepped out of the bathroom and headed for the door to the hall, sending Charlie's heart into his throat.

"Ken," Charlie hissed, moving forward and looking down the dimly lit hallway. "What are you doing?"

Ken quietly twisted the lock on the glass outer door, keeping his nude body out of sight of the hallway. "I'm locking the door. I saw the guy leave."

"What did he look like?" Billy asked, poking his head around the doorframe.

"Couldn't tell." Ken returned to stand before them. "He was dressed in black and was wearing a mask."

"Mask?" Charlie said.

"Yeah." Ken looked him in the eye and Charlie could see how scared he was. "A leather mask with zippers on it, and . . ."

"What?" Charlie asked, swallowing past a lump in his throat.

"There were eyebrows painted on it." Ken ran two fingers across his eyebrows. "Like, you know, the eyebrows Batman has on his mask."

Billy frowned. "Batman doesn't have eyebrows on his mask. He has nipples on his suit, but no eyebrows."

Ken gave him a patient look. He was so young. "Not the movie version Batman, the TV show version." He looked at Charlie. "Remember that? Those white, arched eyebrows?"

Charlie nodded. He remembered watching the TV show reruns when he was a kid and staring at the white, arched eyebrows. But why the hell would eyebrows like that be drawn on a leather S & M mask?

"Come on," Billy said with a shiver. "I want to get out of here."

The three men dressed hurriedly and fled the office, switching off lights behind them. Charlie watched Ken lock the door behind them with a key on his key ring and wondered how many other people had keys to the office. As he rode the bus home, Charlie also wondered who would want to break into Kinitia's office, what they might have been looking for, and why they had an obsession about Adam West's Batman eyebrows.

5

Who Was That Masked Man?

The following week Charlie did not see Rock Harding once. He thought about the man every day, nearly all day, but he did not get to see him. With each assignment Kinitia sent him on, Charlie quietly hoped that Rock would be the one waiting for him, his big, hairless balls swaying between his legs, the long, smooth cock curling up as Charlie started to work. But, all his hoping was for naught. The sets he was sent to included four with bear themes, eight S & M themes, and one young, skateboarder and scooter rider movie. The entire cast of the last movie was younger than Charlie, and probably had more money than he would ever make in his life.

As he closed his eyes and began sucking on the long, young prick before him, Charlie thought about Rock. He missed the solidity of the man, his smell, and the feel of Rock's cock in his mouth.

"Hey, careful fluffer," the young actor snapped. "You're doing it too hard. You don't want me to cum, do you?"

Charlie kept the younger man's cock in his mouth and shook his head. He had gotten worked up over thoughts of Rock and started really sucking his present client. He was going to have to be careful and stop daydreaming at work. Keeping his mind focused, Charlie slowly rode the length of the smooth, pink cock in his mouth. The head was large, rounded, and felt like silk on his tongue.

"That's nice," the actor sighed. "That'll keep me hard for hours."

When Charlie was not providing fluffer service, he was pretty much free to wander around the sets. At the S & M sets, he poked around the prop areas and checked out all the black leather masks with zippers. None of them sported white, arched eyebrows reminiscent of Adam West's Batman.

"What are you doing?" a crewmember asked at one of the sets, walking in on Charlie as he was examining a leather mask.

"Huh? Oh, just looking around." He replaced the mask. "I've never really been into leather or bondage or anything, so I was kind of browsing."

"Oh yeah?" The man leaned back to look up and down the hall behind him, then closed and locked the door. "Want an introductory lesson?"

Charlie narrowed his eyes and assessed the man before him. He was attractive, older than Charlie by about eight years, well-built and undressing Charlie with his eyes. With a nervous shift in his stomach, Charlie shrugged, trying to seem indifferent. "Okay, sure. I'm not due out there for another hour."

A few minutes later, Charlie was nude and kneeling on the floor. His wrists were handcuffed behind him and a tight fitting black leather mask with zippers had been pulled over his head. The only zipper left open by the man, who had introduced himself only as Sir, was the one over Charlie's mouth. A leather cock ring had been wrapped snugly around his cock and balls and tiny clamps were clinging to his nipples. Charlie was rather surprised he wasn't suffering from claustrophobia with the mask fitted tight over his head and the eye holes zippered shut. Other than the rather painful nipple clamps, he thought the whole bondage thing might not be so bad after all.

"Comfy?" Sir asked.

"Yeah, sure," Charlie replied. A sharp sting burned across his bare back. "Ow! What was that?"

"The whip," Sir said. "You did not address me as 'Sir' and so you got the whip. Now, let's try again: Comfy?"

Charlie nodded stiffly. "Yes, Sir."

"Good. Suck my cock."

The man's penis was suddenly crammed into the mouth opening of the mask and barreled past Charlie's lips. He choked around the girth, the man was the size of a nuclear submarine, then closed his eyes in the dark confines of the mask and began to suck.

"Oh, that's it. Suck Sir's cock. Suck it. Yeah, take it all the way down your throat." Sir placed a hand on top of Charlie's leather covered head and began to pump his hips faster.

Charlie tried to bring his hands up to grab the man's cock and stroke it, but he had forgotten he was handcuffed. He shrugged his shoulder muscles back to ease some of the tension and started to really work at Sir's dick. He sucked and licked and tongued the long, thick cock, all the while listening to a steady stream of instructions issued by the man before him.

"Suck Sir's cock. Oh, that's it. Get that tongue up inside Sir's piss slit. Yeah, lick that slit. Get it in there. Drink Sir's pre cum. Oh, yeah. Suck it. Suck it."

Charlie could feel his own cock bouncing with the pulse of his blood. Pre cum was oozing from the head and running down the shaft. He pressed his face forward and swallowed the entire length of the man, tasting the bitter pre cum in the back of his throat.

"Oh, that's nice. Deep throat Sir's big fucking cock. That's right. Take it all the way down. Oh, yeah." Sir kept a hand on Charlie's head and bucked his hips some more. "Take it. Suck it. Get that cum out of my cock. Pull it up out of my balls. Yeah, that's it."

Charlie slobbered and slurped and sucked at Sir's dick. Saliva drooled from his lips and ran down the front of the mask in glistening trails.

"You like that cock in your throat?" Sir asked.

"Mm hmm," Charlie moaned around the meat.

"You want it up your ass?"

"Mm hmm," Charlie moaned with more enthusiasm.

"Come on." Sir removed his cock from Charlie's mouth and pulled him to his feet. "Over here."

Sir unfastened the handcuffs and helped Charlie get up into a leather swing, no mean feat since Charlie was still wearing the leather mask and could not see a thing. Before too long, Charlie's arms were extended above his head and his legs were chained up and spread open. His cock drooled pre cum into a tiny pond that spread beneath the line of hair that ran from his navel to his groin.

A thick finger poked insistently at Charlie's asshole. It massaged the tight, puckered opening and then Sir spit onto it and began moving his finger in tiny circles through the wetness. Before long Sir slipped his finger up into Charlie's ass, twisting and reaching as far up inside him as possible.

"Does that feel good?" Sir asked.

"Oh, yes, Sir," Charlie replied. "That's nice."

"You want more?" Sir asked.

"Yes, Sir, please," Charlie answered, getting a little more into the game.

Sir inserted another finger up alongside the first. He stretched Charlie's sphincter muscle a little wider, then worked a third finger up into him. A short time later, Sir pulled his fingers out and Charlie heard the rustle of a condom wrapper being opened. The fingers were back, this time spreading slick lube around and into his asshole. Charlie groaned and swiveled his hips in the swing.

"Get ready," Sir said and pressed the tip of his cock up against the pink, quivering hole. One thrust was all it took and he was fully embedded in Charlie's body.

"Oh, fuck!" Charlie gasped. He thought the man would never stop invading him. The thick cock filled his body and parted muscle tissue like a skewer. Charlie felt like a human shish kebob.

Sir took hold of Charlie's ankles and slowly began to pump his hips. He slipped almost entirely free of Charlie's anus, then pushed his dick all the way back in. Sensation buzzed through Charlie's head as Sir fucked him harder and harder. His body swung back and forth with the force of the man's thrusts, lending a weightless feel to the act. Charlie swooned a little and felt his cock begin to twitch.

Raising his head, Charlie grunted, "Fuck me harder. I'm cumming."

Sir's pace increased, practically doubled, and his dick began battering Charlie's hole without mercy. With a strangled moan, Charlie blew his wad up over his chest and belly. Not long after that, he felt Sir's cock swell and burst into the condom up inside him. The man grunted with each deep thrust and then leaned his head up against Charlie's leg as he slowly pulled his prick free.

After being helped down, Charlie removed the mask and grinned at the man before him. During sex, the man had seemed much more powerful, more assertive. Now he just looked like any other crewmember on the set of a porn movie.

"Thanks," Sir said with a smirk. "I had a good time."

Charlie smiled. "Me too. See you around."

Sir left the room and Charlie winced as he carefully pulled off the nipple clamps, looking around some more while he cleaned up. Whoever had broken into Kinitia's office had been looking for something. If only he could figure out what that might have been, it would make figuring out who had broken in that much easier.

Charlie worked the rest of the day on the bondage set, fluffing and eavesdropping. With all these leather masks around, someone might slip and mention the break in. He left late that evening with his time card and no information to share with Ken and Billy. He was tired and looking forward to a hot shower and a quiet evening.

Stopping in at the office to drop off his time card, Charlie found Kinitia sitting at the front desk, her head in her heads as she read over a pile of papers in front of her.

"You're here late," Charlie said quietly.

"Yeah, I'm trying to find the last lease agreement I signed with this landlord," Kinitia replied. She was tired and Charlie could see the worry in her eyes. "I keep hearing rumors from the other tenants that the landlord has it in for me or the rent's going up. But I'll be damned if I can figure out why."

Charlie told her about the strange man with the leather mask who had been in the office the week before. Kinitia's face clouded up and her eyes grew cold, making Charlie fear he was about to be fired.

"Why wasn't I told about this last week when it happened?" Kinitia demanded. "I should have been told."

Charlie gulped. "I thought Ken was going to tell you."

"Well, he didn't." She got up to pace the area behind the desk. "Why the hell would someone break in here?"

Charlie stayed with her for almost an hour, making suggestions only to have them shot down. Finally, he took his leave and wished her a good night, heading to the bus stop even more tired than before. As he was waiting for the bus, Ken Carlton and Billy Ransom pulled up to the curb in Ken's red VW Beetle.

"Hey!" Billy called from the window. "Where the fuck are you going?"

"Home!" Charlie stated forcefully. "I'm tired."

"Come with us to a party in the hills," Ken coaxed.

"I'm really tired," Charlie said, but with less determination than before.

"Come on," Billy pleaded. "It'll be fun. It's a big party."

Charlie hesitated, then climbed into the cramped backseat. On the way to the party, he quizzed Ken on his reasoning for not alerting Kinitia to the prowler.

"I didn't want to worry her," he replied. "It didn't look like anything had been taken."

"Could it have been Cedric Wilmington?" Charlie asked.

"The director?" Billy said with a frown. "Why would he want to break in to our offices?"

Ken shook his head and glanced up at Charlie in the mirror. "The guy wasn't built like Cedric. This guy was shorter and in great shape."

Charlie explained the tension between Cedric and Kinitia to Billy and wound up his story just as Ken found a parking spot down the block from a brightly-lit house. They walked up to the house, the sound of music, laughter and an occasional shout growing louder with each step. Inside the crowded living room, beautiful men and women stood and swayed like buoys in a high tide. The conversations merged into one loud drone competing for space in the room beneath the thump of an expensive sound system. Smoke was everywhere and burned into Charlie's eyes as he followed Ken and Billy into the gourmet kitchen. They nodded to some people and grabbed two beers each from ice filled tubs in a corner. Someone was going to a lot of expense to have fun.

"Let's go upstairs and see what's going on!" Ken said into Charlie's ear. He nodded and they headed for the steps leading upstairs as Billy waved to them and followed two well built men down into the basement.

The upstairs held six bedrooms and three bathrooms. Each of the bedrooms was occupied by at least five couples, made up indiscriminately of men and women, all in various stages of undress and copulation. They browsed through each room, walking amid the gasps and groans like weekend antiquaries out looking for a bargain.

After the rounds had been made through the bedrooms, Ken knelt before a handsome male couple who were kissing and petting each other on a chaise lounge. He began tugging at both of their zippers and smirked up at them as the men turned to grin back. Ken produced two long, hardening dicks and leaned down to begin sucking the man on his right, a very tan blonde with a brush cut. The blond man closed his eyes and sighed then turned to his partner, a fair skinned red head, and began to kiss him slowly, passionately. Ken sucked the blond's dick for awhile longer, then shifted position and lowered his mouth over the red head's slightly longer cock which was surrounded by a wiry red bush. Ken took the dick to hilt, his nose brushing against the red head's flat, hairy stomach.

"Oh, yeah," the red head groaned. "Suck that dick."

Ken raised his head and opened his mouth, sticking out his tongue and running it along the ridge beneath the head of the man's dick. He licked slowly up the length of the cock and briefly sucked on just the head as the red head moaned into the blond's mouth. Ken then moved to the right and repeated the process on the blond's cock, taking it completely into his throat and sucking for a time before running his tongue over the entire shaft.

Opening his mouth wider, Ken directed both cocks between his lips and closed his eyes as he massaged each head with his tongue. He swallowed as much of each man as he could, his cheeks bulging with their cocks. With his mouth opened far enough for both men, Ken's saliva ran out over his lower lip and dripped down his chin.

Charlie watched Ken as he deftly sucked both cocks, then turned and headed for a door he hoped was a bathroom. His bladder was painfully full and he had to work down the erection he was sporting after watching Ken's interaction. He knocked tentatively, received no response, and turned the knob. Rock Harding stood before a mirror, peering at himself with narrowed eyes. He looked golden and gorgeous in a casual outfit of jeans and a white cotton shirt.

"Oh! Sorry," Charlie said. "I thought it was empty."

Rock turned quickly, irritated at the intrusion, then his face relaxed and he smiled at the sight of him. "Charlie!"

"Hi," Charlie replied. "I didn't know you would be here."

Rock shrugged. "Cedric wanted to come. He likes to be seen out in public with me."

"Ah. I see." Charlie stood awkwardly against the closed door. "I just needed to use the . . . you know, the bathroom."

"Oh, go ahead," Rock turned back to the mirror. "Don't let me stop you."

Charlie rolled his eyes. He would never be able to piss with Rock standing next to him. He was pee shy enough as it was without being attracted to the person standing beside him. He crossed the room and stood with his back to Rock, pulling out his cock and willing it to soften long enough for him to pee.

"Been here long?" Rock asked, plucking at his hair in the mirror.

"Uh, not really." Charlie willed Rock to be silent for a few minutes so he could pee, but to no avail.

"Come here alone?" Rock asked.

"No. I came with Ken and Billy from work." Charlie turned and smiled at Rock. "They're off mingling." He turned back to face the wall and closed his eyes. He thought of a waterfall, fountains, ice cold tap water, anything to get his bladder to release. It worked. A feeble stream of urine eked out, steadily building to a full release that allowed Charlie to sigh and relax his tensed muscles.

Once he had finished, Charlie tucked himself away, flushed the toilet, and turned to face Rock. The man was leaning back against the counter with his big arms folded over his chest and a small, sexy grin on his face.

"What?" Charlie asked, stopping and looking down. "Did I pee on myself?" He noticed his fly was still open and rolled his eyes.

"No, I was just . . ."

The door burst open and Cedric Wilmington, porn director extraordinaire, incredible he-bitch, and Rock's lover stood in the doorway. He was all false smiles until he caught sight of Charlie zipping up his jeans. His expression darkened so quickly Charlie feared for his life.

"*You!*" Cedric shouted. He barreled across the room and right up into Charlie's face. His breath was horrible: stale beer, scotch, marijuana, and some kind of Mexican dish that washed over Charlie and forced him to recoil.

"What the fuck are you doing in here with my lover?" Cedric stuck a finger in Charlie's face. "You are to stay away from him, do you hear me? I have specifically told all of Rock's directors not to hire any slutty fluffer from Kinitia's company for any of Rock's movies."

"Hey, Cedric," Rock said calmly, laying his big hands on the man's flabby shoulders. "Leave the kid alone. He was just taking a piss. I stayed in here to keep out of the smoke, you know how it affects my sinuses."

Cedric lifted his chin and squared his rounded shoulders as best he could. "All right. But I'm warning you, fluffer: stay away from Rock Harding."

"Come on, Cedric," Rock said with a wink to Charlie. "Let's get out of here. You're drunk and your breath is offensive."

Cedric's eyes widened. "Oh no. Really?" He covered his mouth and hurried from the room.

"Sorry," Rock said to Charlie. "He's drunk."

"Great excuse," Charlie replied. "But it's okay. He's insecure and you mean a lot to him."

Rock shook his head. "I'm a possession he enjoys owning, a decoration, that's all."

"Rock!" Cedric shrieked from the bottom of the stairs. His shrill voice cut through the music and conversation, effectively startling everyone within the confines of the house.

Rock reached out and chucked Charlie beneath the chin. "It was nice to see you again, Charlie. And don't worry about my directors, they use who they want on their sets."

Rock turned and left the room, leaving Charlie dazed and somewhat anxious. What the hell was going on?

As he was washing his hands, the door slammed open again. Charlie jumped clear to the other side of the spacious bathroom, his hands up and ready to defend himself. He was sure Cedric had come back to exact his revenge. But it was simply Billy, looking at him with a puzzled expression.

"Jumpy?" Billy asked.

"Yeah." Charlie dried his hands. "What's up?"

"I think I found the mask." Billy's eyes glowed with excitement. He was living out a Hardy Boys adventure in sunny LA.

Charlie stared at him for a moment. "You're kidding."

"No, I'm not. Come on, I'll show you. Get Ken."

A small crowd had gathered to watch Ken and they had to elbow their way to the front of the half circle. They found Ken stroking and sucking both men simultaneously, his lips puffy and his cheeks bulged out. The men were kissing passionately and tweaking each other's nipples beneath opened shirts.

"Wow, two at once?" Billy said quietly, not wanting to distract Ken.

"Yeah," Charlie replied. "Look at him go."

Ken's fists rode the shafts of each dick, his fingers curled around the tightened, glistening skin as he sucked the tips of both cocks. His eyes were closed and sweat beaded his forehead, evidence of the effort he was putting forth.

"Oh, yeah," the blond gasped. "Oh, uh! Uh!"

Cum filled Ken's mouth and the fluffer kept right on sucking, drawing the rest of the blond's semen out of his dick as his hands stroked both cocks. The red head leaned back against the wall and grunted as his cock exploded into Ken's mouth. More semen spilled out over Ken's lips and down along his chin. He sucked both men for a bit longer, milking the last drops of cum from each, then raised his head and let more semen dribble out of his mouth with a smile.

The blond leaned down and kissed Ken on the mouth, tasting himself and his partner. The red head copied the blond's actions and then the small crowd around the trio gave a polite round of applause and turned to move on to the next scene being enacted across the room.

Ken stood up and turned to Charlie and Billy. "Hi there."

"Wow, impressive," Charlie said. "Two at once."

Ken shrugged. "Not a big deal, really. Just takes practice. Do you know where the bathroom is?"

Charlie led them to the bathroom and he and Billy leaned against the counter as Ken washed up and rinsed out his mouth. When he was drying his face, Billy told him about finding the mask.

"You found it?" Ken said with raised eyebrows. "Where?"

"I'll show you!" Billy led them down the stairs and then the three men descended into the cavernous basement. They followed Billy through rooms with sofas and a big screen TV, two spare bedrooms occupied by a myriad of people, and finally into a cinderblock walled room with a concrete floor containing a sling as well as various implements of sexual arousal. Dildos by the dozen and in varying shapes, sizes, and colors stood stacked on a table along one wall. Another wall supported leather chaps, whips, and manacles.

"Wow, S & M Surplus store," Ken said as he fingered a mammoth dildo. "I think I did a movie with the guy they modeled this dildo after."

"Over here," Billy said in a loud whisper. He was holding up a black leather mask with zippers. They approached him and Ken took the mask, turning to hold it up to the single bare bulb. "See the eyebrows?" Billy asked excitedly.

Ken and Charlie squinted up at the mask, then Ken reached out and scraped off the eyebrows. Smirking, he handed the mask back to Billy and said, "It was dried cum."

"Are you sure?" Billy asked. He held the mask up to his face and sniffed at the spot over the eye zippers.

"I'm sure. If it's one thing I can recognize, it's old spooge." Ken finished buttoning his shirt and stretched. "Well, I'm about ready to call it a night. How about you two?"

"I'm more than ready," Charlie grumped.

They left the house and headed back to the car. Charlie noticed Billy was quiet, disappointed about the dead end they had encountered. He put his arm around the younger man's shoulders and hugged him to his side.

"We'll figure it out," Charlie said. "Don't wish it over yet, there's so much adventure ahead of us. Enjoy the chase."

Billy grinned up at him. "I never thought of it that way."

"Not many people do." Charlie got in the tiny back seat and stretched out, closing his eyes and thinking alternately of Rock Harding and the mysterious masked man. What an interesting week it had been.

6

Trooper Jake and Charlie's Mistake

Charlie squinted from the glare off the sand surrounding him and turned to Billy. "Check the directions again. I think we missed the turn off somewhere."

Billy gave him a lazy look. He was sprawled out in the passenger seat of Ken's Beetle, his feet hanging out the passenger window as the wind buffeted the exterior and whipped scorching heat through the interior of the little car. "We didn't miss the turn off because there hasn't been another road since we left the highway."

Charlie bit back annoyance and said, "Please placate me and check the directions again."

Billy shrugged and went about righting himself. He opened the glove box and the single sheet of notepaper upon which Kinitia had written out the directions was lifted up and sucked out the window by the wind. "Shit!" Billy cried. He turned to look back and watched the paper blow across the dry, cracked asphalt and into the shifting sand beyond the shoulder.

"Tell me that was just an old receipt or something," Charlie said with quiet anger.

Billy looked at him sheepishly. "Sorry."

"God damn it, Billy!" Charlie took a breath and calmed himself down. "Okay, it's okay. We'll just turn around and go back."

He slowed down and swung the small car around, easing along the road until he came to a cactus he thought he recognized from when the directions had blown away. How ironic, he thought as he slowed the car to a stop on the shoulder. Two cocksuckers trying to get to a porn set in the desert and the directions are sucked out the window.

They got out into the heat and began to walk through the sand, kicking at litter and other debris. It was no use. The paper was gone. Charlie stood beneath the burning sun with sand in his shoes and his hands on his hips, turning his face up to the incredibly blue sky and wondering how to get them out of this mess. He had no cell phone, not that it would work out here anyway, and half a tank of gas. The air conditioning in Ken's Beetle was on the fritz and they had two bottles of water.

That was when the big police cruiser pulled up behind the Beetle and switched on its flashers.

Charlie shook his head. "Probably get a ticket for something to top it all off."

"Oh, wow," Billy gasped, his eyes on the cop stepping out of the cruiser.

Charlie turned and felt his mouth go even drier. The cop was tall and muscular with a square jaw, broad chest, and narrow hips. He walked around the front of his car and leaned back against the quarter panel, crossing his arms and nearly tearing through the short sleeves of his uniform. Charlie felt his cock spring to life at the sight of the hot rock of a trooper standing before him and knew Billy was just as hard.

"Problem gentlemen?" The trooper's voice was deep and throaty, a voice made to shout out commands during sex.

"We lost our directions," Billy said. "It got sucked out the window."

The trooper eyed the Beetle through his mirrored sunglasses. "No AC?"

Charlie shook his head. "System leak."

"Not the best day to drive through the desert with no AC." The trooper turned to look Charlie square in the face. "Where are you trying to get to?"

Charlie wondered how much to tell this guy. He could be a friendly, helpful trooper, or he could be a gay bashing psychopath.

Before Charlie could decide what to tell the man, Billy piped up and said, "A movie set. We're part of the crew."

"I don't recall a movie being filmed around here. What's the title?"

Charlie and Billy exchanged a look. Should they tell him? Charlie decided to start with the truth, it was always easier to remember what you told people that way. "*Anally Yours.*"

The trooper's mouth twitched into a grin. "Really? And two attractive young men like you are only part of the crew? I would have thought you'd at least have minor roles." He straightened up. "Let me check and see if we have any permits pulled."

He got back in the car and spoke into the microphone. Charlie and Billy walked up and leaned against the dusty surface of the Beetle, both sweating profusely in the glare of the sun. A few minutes later the trooper was back outside and leaning against the front of his cruiser.

"There's an independent production going on in the mesas a few miles back. The turn off is a dirt road, that's probably why you missed it." He looked at Charlie. "Who was driving?"

Charlie raised his hand, slightly embarrassed although not knowing why. "I was."

"No sunglasses?" the cop asked.

"They broke yesterday and I haven't had a chance to buy any others." He shrugged. "Well, thanks for the information, officer, uh . . . ?"

"Benton. Jake Benton." He stood up to his full height of at least six foot five and let his arms hang at his sides. His hands were huge, covered with dark hair that traveled up his forearms. "Look, if you want I can escort you back to the road."

"Oh, well, that won't be necessary . . ." Charlie let his voice trail off.

"Is there any way we can thank you for your help?" Billy asked, smiling at the big cop.

"Well, I have been a little tense today." The cop reached down and gently squeezed his crotch. "I could use a little relaxation before my shift ends, if you know what I mean." He grinned and a mouth full of white teeth dazzled Charlie. What did people in California brush with, bleach?

They moved to the desert side of the cruiser and Jake opened the back door. They slid in, leaving the door open, and Charlie leaned into the big man stretched out beneath him, kissing him deeply and squeezing his hard chest beneath the uniform. Billy ran his tongue along the solid length of Jake's arm, sucking each finger on his hand. The cop moaned beneath their administrations and the men began to unbutton his shirt, eager to get a look at his body.

Before long the three of them were nude. Jake had a layer of dark hair over his body, a detail that Charlie committed to memory for masturbation fantasies in the future. He loved hairy men. The smell of Jake's sweat slithered into their nostrils and fueled their dicks to complete erection. Charlie moved his mouth down over Jake's flat stomach and to the perfectly shaped navel partially hidden by hair. He slipped his tongue into the tiny cave of skin and looked down at the thick cock staring up at him. It lay on Jake's groin and belly like a forgotten club, fat and hard.

"Oh, that feels good," Jake groaned as Billy ran his tongue along the trooper's thigh and up to his balls. Jake spread his legs open, the black boots he had pulled back on bumping against the open door. Billy licked and sucked on Jake's balls, lapping up the layers of work sweat that had built up over the course of the man's shift. "Yeah, suck those balls. Get 'em in your mouth. Yeah, that's it."

Charlie moved to the head of Jake's cock, running his tongue around the edges of the beast where it lay on his stomach, like a detective using chalk to outline a body. The dense smell of sweat invaded his senses as he buried his nose and mouth in the sensitive area of Jake's pubic bush. He kissed and sucked at the skin, brushing his cheek up against the hard cock next to his face.

"Oh, God," Jake groaned. He laid his head back, sunlight glinting off the lenses of the sunglasses he still wore. "That feels really good. Oh, yeah." He pressed a hand to the back of Charlie's head and mashed his face further into the pubic hair. "Lick that bush."

Charlie sucked at the skin, then moved up along the length of Jake's dick and teased the very tip of his cock with his tongue. He tasted pre cum and moved his head back, taking a strand of the shimmering fluid with him. When the string broke, Charlie lifted Jake's member and lowered his mouth over the length of the cock. His nose bumped up against the soft cushion of Jake's big balls which rested on Billy's face. Billy was presently rimming Jake's asshole, licking and sucking at the trooper's anus.

"Oh, fuck!" Jake grunted as Charlie swallowed his dick. "Yeah, suck that big cop cock. Eat my ass and suck my cock, yeah, that's it."

Billy was eating Jake's ass with abandon, slurping and sucking at the twitching pucker. Charlie began sucking Jake's cock, rising and falling more rapidly each time. As he worked the cop's dick, Charlie felt Jake wrap a big hand around his own cock and begin to stroke. Charlie moaned down into the fur surrounding Jake's groin as he deep throated the man again.

"Get a dick up my ass," Jake said. "Suck my cock and fuck my ass."

Billy pulled a lubricated condom from his jeans lying crumpled on the floor of the cruiser and rolled it over his cock. Lifting Jake's ankles, he moved up to press himself against the cop's anxious hole and squeezed his length of hardness completely into the man. Charlie continued to suck Jake's dick as Billy began to batter away at his ass. The cop's boots hung in the air, bouncing with each thrust of Billy's hips.

"Yeah, ride that fuckin' ass," Jake instructed. "Get it up in there. Come on, plow that ass. Oh, yeah. Fill my ass with your cock."

Billy picked up his pace and his balls began slapping audibly against the crack of Jake's ass as he pounded into the big man. Charlie increased the rate of his sucking, wrapping his hand around the glistening shaft and moving up to focus on the sensitive cap.

"Oh, fuck!" Jake's mouth dropped open in a soundless cry. Charlie lifted his mouth just as the first burst of cum shot out of Jake's cock. The semen splashed across his chin and lips. The smell immediately brought him close to the edge as he pumped the rest of Jake's load out of his cock and onto his face. The cum dripped from Charlie's jaw to Jake's flat, sweaty stomach where it sank through the hair to rest on his skin.

Billy pulled his cock out of Jake's ass and stripped off the condom. The cop slid out of the back seat and knelt on a cushion of clothes on the gravel shoulder with his face turned up, fondling himself. He sucked their cocks until both men took themselves in hand and brought on orgasms. Billy shot seconds before Charlie, his cum landing in a line up the length of Jake's face and tangling in his short cropped dark hair. A large glob of the stuff hit smack dab in the center of the left lens of his sunglasses. Charlie's load took over the lower half of Jake's face, covering his nose, lips, and chin.

When they had finished, Billy and Charlie used their softening cocks to smear the cum around Jake's face. The cop groaned beneath them, his face covered with their spunk.

Jake got up and pulled out a wet wipes dispenser from the front seat. They all cleaned up then got dressed. As Billy and Charlie headed to the car, Jake called out, "Hey, driver."

Charlie turned and shielded his eyes against the sun. "Yeah?"

"Here." Jake walked up and placed his mirrored sunglasses on Charlie's face. Charlie looked up into Jake's bright blue eyes and smiled. The spot of Billy's cum blurred the vision of his left eye just a little.

"Thanks, but what about you?"

"I've got another pair in the car. Follow me and I'll lead you to that turn off."

Twenty minutes later, after waving good bye to Jake, Charlie bounced the Beetle around a set of tall mesas and came upon several trucks and a trailer. Cameras were set up around a rock wall to frame a scene. At the moment no filming was being done.

Charlie and Billy approached a crewmember and asked to see the director. Charlie recognized the man the crewmember pointed out as Rod, the director from the last time he had worked with Rock Harding in the cabin near the waterfall. Perfect. Maybe the man wouldn't remember how he had bitten Rock's dick when his chair collapsed.

"Oh, it's Jaws," Rod quipped as they approached him. "This should be fun. Try to keep my actors intact, okay?"

Charlie chuckled in a good-natured way, but inside he was rankled. Like he could have known the chair would collapse. Rod shooed them away; he was trying to set up a shot and would let them know when they were needed.

Billy and Charlie found places to sit in the shade and grabbed some water bottles from a cooler. They waited. And they waited. And they waited. The sun moved to directly overhead, obliterating all hopes of finding shade. And then Rod decided to film at the top of one of the mesas.

Two men were sent up a steep, crumbling path to look the site over. They came back with good news: it could work and provide a spectacular vista of the desert in the background. Equipment was packed and lugged up the path and soon Charlie and Billy were sitting on rocks atop the flat mesa almost two hundred feet in the air. The sides of the tower were steep and only one path provided access. Charlie avoided looking over the edge as his fear of heights gave him vertigo whenever he looked straight down.

Charlie was so tense about the physical location he did not notice the actors walking up the path. All of them were bitching about the climb. Their hair was fried by the sun or they were hung over from their parties the night before. One of them was applying Vaseline to a brand new tattoo.

And at the back of the pack, his head slowly rising up from behind the rocks by the path, came Rock Harding. He was wearing white boxer briefs and hiking boots. His leg muscles defined themselves with each step he took and Charlie noticed he had stopped breathing at the sight of the man. Rock was so physically striking it was impossible not to stare.

Rock paused at the top of the path to catch his breath, then turned to look out over the expanse of desert. Charlie realized that out of all the people up on the mesa only Rock, Billy, Rod, and himself had stopped to take in the scenery. The other actors had made a beeline for the folding chairs beneath beach umbrellas and coolers of cold beer and water.

"Okay, fluffers on your mark," Rod said with a grin. "This is a group shot and I need all eight of these ladies up and ready to go in fifteen minutes. Light and money is wasting."

Charlie and Billy got down on their knees, using cushions to keep from injuring themselves on the gravel. The actors all gathered around, four to each, and dropped their briefs.

Looking around, Charlie noticed Rock walking up to Billy's side of the line and felt his heart drop. A cock slapping across his cheek, however, brought him back to the matter at hand and he began to suck and stroke the dicks before him.

As they were serviced, the actors chatted with each other about dates and parties, reminding Charlie of old women under hair dryers in a beauty shop. He grinned around a mouthful of hardening dick as the image expanded to these pretty boys sitting under big pink dryers and filing their nails or flipping through magazines as they gossiped.

The dicks were stiffening nicely, getting ready for the big scene, when suddenly a new cock appeared in his peripheral vision. Charlie released an almost fully erect dick from his mouth, continued stroking two others, and turned to take the new cock between his lips. Glancing up just as he felt the tip brush against his tongue, Charlie found Rock Harding gazing intently down at him. Charlie smiled and blushed as Rock winked.

"Okay, where are the first two?" Rod called. Two men broke away, both from Billy's group, and one of Charlie's men moved over to let Billy have a go. Charlie continued to move from prick to prick, stroking those that he was not sucking, but he seemed to keep coming back to fluff Rock's beautiful dick more often.

The scene behind them was filmed at the edge of the mesa with the desert laid out in the background. The first two actors, both blond with firm, smooth bodies, stood kissing a safe distance back from the ledge. Their tongues slopped spit over their lips and chins as they kissed and licked at one another. One of the men, the taller of the two, lifted the other's arm and moved down to run his tongue through the neatly trimmed dark blond hair of the exposed armpit. His partner groaned and closed his eyes as the taller man licked and sucked on the hollow of his pit.

Moving lower, the taller actor was soon kneeling before his partner and sucking his long, eight-inch cock with gusto. He drew back until the ridge of the head was exposed between his lips then slid down onto the rigid pole once again, orally impaling himself. With one hand the actor tugged on his partner's balls, a large, smoothly shaved set that hung low between his legs, and with his other hand the actor stroked himself.

"Good!" Rod called out. "Nice action. Okay, where are the next two?"

Two more actors moved off to join the fray. Charlie lost both this time and now had only Rock and another man to work on. Billy was holding his own with three.

The two new actors stepped in behind each of the previous actors. The blond receiving the blowjob leaned back against the new arrival, a slightly hairy brunette, and began to kiss him. The other recent addition stood on the other side of the kneeling actor and stroked himself until the tall, blond man turned and opened his mouth to begin sucking the newly arrived dick.

The kneeling blond man slowly deep throated the cocks before him, swiveling his head to work on each man in turn. Saliva dripped from the blunted heads of whichever dick he released from his mouth before turning to take in the other. He had a hand wrapped around the base of both men's cocks, stroking the man he was not sucking. His own prick stood straight up along his belly, red and nearly bursting with blood as pre cum oozed out of the slit and drizzled down the shaft.

Charlie and Billy were soon down to one actor apiece, and Charlie had Rock. They didn't speak, Charlie just worked his mouth along the long shaft. He sucked and stroked and tugged on Rock's bull balls, keeping his head movements long and slow so as not to bring him to climax.

"Okay, I need the last two," Rod called.

Billy's actor turned and walked away without a word, leaving the fluffer in mid suck. Rock, however, placed his hand softly on the back of Charlie's head and buried the length of his erection in Charlie's throat. They looked into each other's eyes for a moment, then Rock slowly withdrew and turned away, trailing a finger along

Charlie's jaw and wiping up a line of spit from beneath his lips. As Rock headed into the mass of bodies, Charlie saw the actor raise those fingers to his mouth and suck the saliva from them.

Rock walked right into the middle of the group, his dick standing out and commanding attention. He put a hand beneath the jaw of an actor standing bent over and pulled his head back to plant a deep, invasive kiss on his mouth. While kissing the actor, Rock pressed the fat head of his dick against the man's tight, pulsing asshole. Another actor, already on his knees, moved off the dick he was sucking and pulled Rock's organ from between the firm, tan buttocks and began to suck it. Rock moaned and pulled his mouth up from the other man's to look down at the man beneath him.

"Oh yeah," Rock grunted. "Take that cock down your throat. Suck it down."

The other six men gathered around Rock and his partner, making them the center of the orgy. One actor knelt behind Rock and began to perform a deep, wet rim job. Rock bent forward over the man sucking his dick, allowing the man behind him to get deeper up his ass. This position also gave Rock access to his oral worshipper's asshole and he began to eagerly probe the opening with his fingers.

Another actor stepped up and offered his dick for Rock to suck. This actor straddled the oral worshipper's back and, as Rock swallowed his long, vein covered cock, the actor reached out to run his hands over the muscles standing out in Rock's back.

Charlie groaned quietly at the intensity of the scene and stood up. He was hard and wet, pre cum leaking through the material of his jeans. How did the cameramen manage to keep their hands off their dicks while they filmed these scenes?

Soon Rock was in the middle of a chain of anal intercourse. He had his cock stuffed up inside one actor while another fucked him up the ass. Behind Rock's invader another actor had begun fucking that man's ass while two others stood to the side waiting their turn. At the front of the line, the man Rock was fucking was bent over with a dick down his throat.

Charlie made a deep, guttural sound of lust and felt himself sway on his feet a bit. Probably all the blood rushing from his head to his crotch. He stepped back to find his rock again and sit down and knocked up against a light stand, causing it to topple over onto a row of deck chairs. The chairs collapsed in a slow motion domino effect that would have been comical had it been in a movie or happening to someone else. The chairs knocked against another light on a tripod which fell over and promptly exploded, overloading the breaker the crew had lugged to the top of the mesa and killing the power to each piece of equipment. The lights went out, plunging the scene into darkness just as the cum shots began to fly and Rod started screaming in frustration.

After shouting into Charlie's face for thirty minutes, Rod stormed off down the path to his trailer below. The actors had all wandered away, grinning as they passed Charlie and the director. The breaker was reset and the debris from the broken light cleaned up, but the damage had been done. The light was quickly fading. They would need to spend the night and finish the movie in the morning.

Charlie and Billy were ordered to stay and assist in the morning free of charge. Not only would they be fluffers, they would also be acting as part of the crew. After calling Ken on a borrowed cell phone with a surprisingly clear connection, they headed for the Beetle and tried to make themselves comfortable in the fold down passenger seats. It was going to be a very long night.

7

Cedric Carrington-Colby-Wilmington

Charlie could not get comfortable in the driver's seat of the VW Beetle. He tossed and turned but it was no use. He would never be able to sleep inside the car. Billy was curled up on the passenger seat snoring softly as Charlie quietly stepped out of the car. He shivered in the cold night air and looked around. The moon was full, hanging over the production site like an ornamental china plate on a suburban housewife's dining room wall. It spread an eerie white glow over the desert landscape around him and illuminated Charlie's way to the path leading to the top of the mesa.

As he carefully ascended the loose rock and dirt path, Charlie briefly recalled how he had knocked over the light stand and blown out the circuit on the mesa top. When was his luck going to change? Would it ever? How could one young kid from a farm in Idaho cause so many problems on the sets of porn movies in California?

He reached the flat top of the mesa and walked to within ten feet of the edge. His fear of heights kept him from approaching any closer, but the cold, quiet beauty of the landscape below urged him nearer. The desert was spread out before him in a glow of blue and white light. The mesas and undulating hills of sand and rock stretched off into the dark horizon. The sight was breathtaking. And cold. The temperature had plummeted since the sun had gone down and now Charlie wished he had brought a sweatshirt or jacket with him.

"Nice view, isn't it?"

Charlie jumped and turned with his heart in his mouth. It was Rock Harding, standing in the white light with his sexy smile that was such a danger to Charlie's sensibilities. Rock had followed him up the path.

"You scared me," Charlie said. He moved toward Rock and away from the edge of the mesa, suddenly nervous and not trusting himself near such a steep drop, especially with this man around.

"Sorry." Rock was wearing jeans, a light jacket, and a flannel shirt. "I couldn't sleep so I thought I would come up and look around." He moved past Charlie and gazed out over the landscape. "It's amazing, isn't it?"

Charlie smiled. "Yeah, it is. We don't have places like this back in Idaho."

"That's right," Rock said and turned back to him. "I remember you telling me about the farm during dinner. It sounds like a nice place."

Charlie shrugged. "It is. I just wanted to get out and see the world. You can only buy so many gay porn videos out of magazines and not want to come to California." He shivered and rubbed his arms.

"Oh, you must be freezing." Rock pulled off his jacket and held it out. "Take it. I've got a flannel shirt."

"Thanks." Charlie pulled the jacket on and tried not to be too obvious as he breathed in Rock's citrus scent from the collar. The sleeves were too long, making him feel like a kid playing dress up and the lining was warm from Rock's body. Charlie burrowed into the jacket and sighed. "Oh, much better."

"Here, zip up." Rock stepped up to him and pulled the zipper slowly up the length of Charlie's torso, stopping just below his neck. Raising his eyes, Rock looked into Charlie's and said quietly, "I wouldn't want you to catch cold out here. Who would fluff me up in the morning?"

Charlie blushed, hating himself for it, and looked away. "Oh, Billy could do it, I'm sure."

"Not as good as you." Rock still held the tab of the zipper. "You really have a way with your mouth and tongue, Charlie Heggensford."

Charlie blinked at him. Rock Harding had remembered his last name. And said it correctly! "You remember my last name?"

Rock shrugged. "It stands out."

Charlie laughed. "Yeah, it does." He looked around Rock's big biceps and caught a glimpse of movement out on the desert floor. "What was that?"

They approached the edge carefully and both men squinted down onto the land below. Small, skittish shapes darted in and out among the shadows.

"Coyotes," Rock said. "Scavengers."

"Oh. Are they dangerous?" Charlie watched the dogs as they searched for food.

"Not really. Pretty much scared of their own shadows, but I wouldn't suggest cornering one to find out." Rock stepped back a few paces and sat with his back against a large rock. "Hey, come here and join me."

Charlie hesitated. "I dunno. At that party Cedric made it pretty clear I wasn't to be anywhere near you ever again."

Rock grimaced and waved a hand. "Cedric's a tired old queen who doesn't like to be outdone. I make my own decisions and decide who my friends are. Now, come over here and sit by me and we can keep each other warm."

Charlie sat next to the big man and felt Rock's arm slide around his shoulders. He leaned into Rock's armpit and chest and fought back a contented sigh. He felt warmer already.

"Truth is, Cedric and I haven't slept together for over three years," Rock said quietly. "He used to be more easy going and fun to be around, but now he's just this evil bitch no one can seem to stand."

"Why don't you leave?" Charlie asked, somehow fearing the answer.

Rock shrugged and Charlie sensed some tension spring up in the arm around his shoulder. "It's kind of a long story. He treats me okay when we're alone. And I really love the house. I guess

I've just been lazy and stuck in a rut. I mean, I have plenty of sex, on the set and off, and I make enough money to be able to live comfortably, but it's just easier to stay there. It just never really seemed to be an issue. Until now."

Charlie caught the last two words and held them in his heart, treasuring them and wondering just what Rock had meant by them. Could Rock be alluding to an attraction he was harboring for him, unlucky Charlie Heggensford from Idaho? He was afraid to say anything else for fear of breaking the spell that had been cast, but if he didn't acknowledge the cryptic message, would Rock think he wasn't interested? Charlie battled mentally with himself and finally, worn out from running all possible scenarios and outcomes through his mind, wound up keeping quiet.

Both men yawned and shifted positions on the stony ground. The moonlight covered them and lulled them to sleep where they sat atop the mesa.

The next morning a loud, shrieking voice awoke them. Charlie started and sat up, his back stiff and his ass numb from sitting on the hard, cold ground all night. He had a sour taste in his mouth and could feel a tingling in his face from where one of Rock's shirt buttons had left an impression on his cheek. He stretched his mouth in a yawn and turned away to keep from subjecting Rock to his breath.

"Oh, fuck," Rock groaned. He stretched his arms out over his head and twisted his neck from side to side. "I feel like we fell off this fucking thing last night."

Charlie chuckled sleepily. "Me too." He rose unsteadily to his feet and wiped sleep from his eyes. Trying not to be too obvious, he watched Rock stand up slowly and stretch his muscles, working up the blood flow as he reached for the brightening sky and then down to touch the stones at his feet. The man's ass was a thing of beauty beneath the worn, dirty denim of his jeans. Charlie observed it leisurely then fought back a whispering hard-on and headed for the path. Beneath them the shrieking was still going on.

"What the fuck is that noise?" Rock grumbled. He was right behind Charlie, both men carefully picking their way down the path. At the bottom, they stepped out from the side of the mesa and stopped at the same time the shrieking fell silent.

Cedric Wilmington stood at the entrance to one of the actors' trailers, his hands on his ample hips and a big sun hat on his head. His mouth was hanging open as he watched Charlie and Rock stumble sleepily off the path from the top of the mesa.

"Oh, for fuck's sake," Rock muttered. He walked around Charlie and angrily approached Cedric. "What the fuck are you doing here?"

"Well, I might think the line of questioning could be reversed," Cedric snapped. "What the fuck are you doing here?"

"Trying to make a movie," Rock replied.

"Oh? One of your own, or the one you signed up for?" Cedric looked pointedly at Charlie over Rock's shoulder, then turned to the sleepy eyed director who had been roused from his SUV. "What the fuck is that little bitch fluffer doing on your set? I thought I told you not to use that bitch Kinitia's trade any longer?"

Rod glared at Cedric and folded his arms. "First of all, Cedric, you're on my set and you have not been invited. Second of all, I'll use whomever I damn well want on my cast and my crew and nothing you say can or will change that. Now, you're disrupting my actors and the star of my picture and hindering the continuation of my movie. Get your fat ass off my set or I'll call the cops and have you escorted away."

Cedric's face turned a frightening shade of scarlet as he glared at Rod. "You haven't heard the last of this, Rod."

"Ah, go away you tired old has been. I'm sick of your drama." Rod turned his back and walked away. "Everyone up and ready to film in thirty minutes."

Cedric lifted his chin and turned back to Rock. "We'll discuss this at length when you get home." He glared at Charlie over Rock's shoulder, then stomped off to his urine yellow Blazer.

Rock walked up to Charlie and looked down at his feet, clearly embarrassed. "I'm sorry about that. I had no idea he might show up."

Charlie shrugged, trying not to let Rock know how frightened he was of Cedric. He wasn't used to people hating him. "That's okay. I think I understand why he's like that."

"Yeah? Well, you can explain it to me sometime." Rock grinned at him and Charlie grinned back. He remembered the jacket and started to unzip it. "No, keep it," Rock said. "It looks good on you."

"Oh, Rock, I couldn't," Charlie replied.

"Please, just keep it. You can return it the next time we watch the moon over the desert." Rock smiled at him, seemed about to lean forward, then abruptly turned and walked away.

"Okay, well," Charlie said to himself. "I guess I'm more confused than ever now." He walked off to find Billy and then both men began helping with set up. Before long, they were back on top of the mesa, sucking and stroking the actors as the cameras were readied.

Charlie tried not to show favoritism to Rock, but each time he opened his mouth and took in the man's dick, Rock's hips started to pump just slightly and he found he couldn't let him go. Charlie tried to remember to back away from the man when he started to move his hips, but it was difficult.

One by one the actors were called off to perform their roles and soon Billy was fluffing one attractive, blond surfer dude and Charlie was keeping Rock's dick erect. Charlie slid his mouth slowly along the fully engorged shaft, savoring the taste and trying not to focus too much on the man attached to the cock. He was, however, painfully erect himself, his cock trapped in the tangle of his underwear and jeans. Pre cum was soaking through the cotton of his underwear and coming dangerously close to spotting the crotch of his pants.

"Okay, I need the last two," Rod called out. The surfer dude leaned down and kissed Billy quickly on the mouth, then smiled at him and walked away, his cock bobbing before him in all its glory. Rock slowly disengaged from Charlie's mouth, their eyes locked as his dick eased out from between the fluffer's swollen lips. He touched the tip of his dick briefly to Charlie's lips for a final, soft kiss, then winked and turned to walk to the set.

"You are so taken with him it's disgusting," Billy said.

"What?" Charlie said. "Oh, look who's talking. Rock didn't kiss me on the mouth before he left."

"He may as well have," Billy said. "You had better be careful with that, Charlie. Cedric seems like a powerful man in this industry."

"Cedric is a zeppelin, full of hot air and not much else." Charlie turned to watch the scene which had been rewritten by Rod the night before. For fear of causing another accident he remained sitting on the ground.

The men were all gathered in a line with their backs to each other. The man in the front was bent over and stroking himself as the man behind him fucked him. This second man was being fucked by a third, who was being fucked by the fourth, who was being fucked by Rock, and so on. The actors stood in a long, sweating, pumping line as they fucked each other. At first the rhythm was off: one man would be pulling out as his partner did, lessening the length of dick that was visible to the cameras sweeping back and forth. But soon they all fell into rhythm and pumped forward when the dick buried tight up their ass pulled back.

Each man groaned and bucked his hips, driving deep into the clenching hole before him as his own asshole was spread open and penetrated by the man behind. Several of the men gripped the actor before him at the hips, pulling their willing bodies back as they squeezed their thick cocks between the firm, tanned ass cheeks. Sweat ran down their faces and glistened over their chests and backs.

"Okay, remember to keep the cum shots in the correct order!" the director shouted. "This is important!"

The actor at the front of the line, with a six and a half inch long, two inch thick cock slamming up his ass, bit his lower lip and stiffened his legs. His strokes slowed along his cock and his fingers tightened just beneath the head as he brought himself to orgasm. He fired his load high in the air, a camera close to the ground catching the thick wads of semen as they pulsed from his dick. The man milked the last few drops from his cock and bent lower to catch his breath as the actor behind him continued to hammer at his stretched asshole.

"Oh, yeah," the second actor moaned. "I'm cumming!"

The first actor waited until the man pulled completely out of his body, then turned and knelt before him with his face upturned. The second man blew his load over the first actor's face, applying layer after layer of hot, thick cum to the man's tanned features. As his orgasm faded, the first actor opened his mouth and sucked the remaining drops of cum from the second actor's softening dick.

Behind the second actor, the third actor continued to fuck until he got to the edge of his own orgasm. The second actor mimicked the first and turned to kneel with his face raised and his eyes closed as the third actor loosed his load over his forehead, nose, and chin.

The cum shots continued in this fashion through Rock and on to the end of the line. Rock unleashed a virtual flood of semen over the face of the man kneeling at his feet, practically drowning the actor in his bodily fluid. The actor, one of the original blonds who started the scene, smiled up at Rock after he had finished and reached out to fondle his wilting erection, planting a kiss on the slippery, cum smeared tip. Rock then rode out the man behind him until turning and kneeling to receive the brunt of the actor's orgasm. Rock's face was spattered with jism; it streaked over his cheeks and nose and dripped off his jaw.

The final actor came onto the face of the man he had been fucking and Rod had the camera zoom in for a close up of the final dripping cock before he called, "Cut!" The actors got to their feet as assistants handed them towels and the set was struck with surprising efficiency.

Charlie helped to pack up lights and cables, turning to look for Rock as he stowed equipment. The actor was nowhere to be seen and he felt his heart drop a little. How did Rock manage to vanish so quickly from the sets of all his movies? As Charlie rolled up a length of microphone cabling, Rod approached him.

"Charlie, right?"

"Uh, yeah." Charlie carefully set down the microphone and cable he was holding.

"I just wanted to apologize for shouting at you yesterday," Rod continued. "I was tired and a little stressed and when you blew out the power I went a little over the top."

"Oh, well, thanks, but I did kind of deserve it."

"Not that much. Any way, the shots from this morning look even better than what I was getting last night, and I had a chance to rewrite the final sequence so it really kind of worked out for the best." Rod looked around, almost nervously. "Well, to show my appreciation, I'd like to pay you and Billy for your work today and take you to dinner."

Charlie smiled. "Wow, that would be great. I know Billy would like to go to dinner, he hasn't been able to afford a nice dinner . . ."

Rod held up a hand. "Actually, I was thinking of just you and me going to dinner."

Charlie blinked. "Oh. Well, um, yeah, that would be good."

"If you don't want to go, just say so and I'll understand," Rod replied.

Charlie looked up at him and noticed again how handsome the director was with dark wavy hair, mustache, and brown eyes. "No, it would be nice."

Rod smiled. "Good. Tomorrow night okay?"

Charlie nodded. "Yeah, tomorrow night would be great."

Rod took down Charlie's phone number and descended the path to the trailer below. Charlie completed packing up his portion of the equipment and loaded it in the truck at the base of the mesa. After having their time cards signed by Rod, Billy and Charlie got into Ken's Beetle and headed back to the city. He did not see Rock at all before they left the movie site.

After running the VW through a quick car wash to get the desert dust off, they parked it in the lot for the offices of Fluffers, Inc. and headed for the door. Kinitia was sitting at her desk in the reception area and smiled at their tan faces. "You boys look young and beautiful."

Billy smiled. "And horny as hell after two days of sucking porn star cock." He strutted off to the rest room, leaving Charlie and Kinitia grinning at each other.

"How did it go?" Kinitia asked.

Charlie handed her their time cards. "I got asked out to dinner."

Kinitia's face froze. "You did? Who asked you out? Please tell me it wasn't Rock Harding."

Charlie shifted his weight nervously, saying with a defensive edge to his voice, "No. It wasn't Rock. It was Rod Mandrake, the director."

Kinitia breathed a sigh of relief. "Thank God. I don't want any more shit from that bitch Cedric."

"Too late for that, honey," a low, sinister voice said from over Charlie's shoulder.

He turned to find Cedric Wilmington standing just inside the door of Fluffers, Inc. The sun hat was still perched on his head, the brim circling his skull like the rings of Saturn. He wore large dark glasses, a loose fitting silk shirt and pants, and some sort of open toed wing tip. He looked like an example of bad Joan Collins drag. Cedric smiled, his soft, pasty face pulling up with the effort. "I just wanted to stop by and wish my newest tenant good luck."

Kinitia narrowed her eyes. "What are you talking about?"

Cedric's smile dropped and he reached up to remove his sunglasses, exposing his beady and faded blue eyes. "I just bought controlling interest from the owner of this building. As of this morning I am the new owner of your office space. You can expect your rent to triple, at the very least. Good luck making your payments. If you miss one payment, just one, I'll see to it that you and your nasty little harem of bitches and fags are tossed out on your whoring asses so fast you won't know what hit you."

With a soft whisk of silk, Cedric spun on his heel and left the office, some designer knock off scent wafting behind him. Charlie clenched his teeth and turned to Kinitia. She was sitting with her head in her hands and a panicked look on her face.

"What am I going to do?" Kinitia asked. "Why is he so hell bent on putting me out of business?"

Charlie cleared his throat and she slowly raised her head to take in his guilty expression. "You? But, I thought Rod Mandrake asked you out?"

"He did," Charlie replied. "But Rock and I sort of fell asleep together up on top of a mesa."

"*What?*" Kinitia shouted and sprang to her feet. "You *slept* with the man?"

"Yes!" Charlie said. The other fluffers were coming up front from the back room, drawn to the tone and volume of Kinitia's voice. "Sort of. We just fell asleep together. There was no sex involved."

Kinitia reached out and slapped Charlie on the side of his head. "You are still just a farm fresh egg out here, you know that? This industry is built on people having sex. Anonymous sex, casual sex, sex on film, sex for money, it's all based on sex. Sex is an everyday occurrence to these people. But just "sleeping together" without having sex is a much more intimate and threatening act. Don't you get it? You've gotten to Rock Harding more than Cedric ever could. Sure, Rock had sex with Cedric, but he never spent the night on top of a desert mesa with him!" Kinitia took a breath and put her hands on the back of her head, looking up at the ceiling and breathing deeply. "This is going to be a problem."

"I'm sorry," Charlie mumbled, avoiding the eyes of the rest of the fluffing team. "I didn't realize."

Kinitia looked at him for a moment, then rounded the desk and pulled him to her in a hug. "I know you didn't. But you've got to start being careful around this guy. You can't avoid him if he's working on a movie, but leave him alone otherwise. Okay?" Charlie nodded and fought back his tears. He would never make it in this business. Kinitia smoothed his hair back from his forehead and smiled at him. "Go home and get some rest. I've got some assignments for you tomorrow."

Charlie nodded and left the office, wiping his eyes.

Ken Carlton herded the rest of the fluffers back to the waiting room then returned to the front. He crouched before the desk and rested his chin on the edge. "What are you going to do?"

Kinitia shrugged. "What can I do? I'll try to make the rent however I can."

"I've got some money saved up," Ken said. "I can help out. And I can start doing the escort thing again."

Kinitia reached out and ran her fingers through his hair. "I won't take you up on that yet, but maybe later. Thanks."

"It will be okay, Kinitia," Ken said as convincingly as possible. She smiled, but he could tell from her eyes that she wasn't convinced.

8

And The Nominees Are...

Charlie waited in front of his building for Rod Mandrake. It was their first date and he had no intention of allowing Rod to see the size or condition of his apartment. He checked his watch and looked up and down the street again. No sign of the director. Maybe he had forgotten? Or maybe Cedric had threatened him as well?

Moments later, a long black Town Car pulled up at the curb and the passenger window hummed down. The driver, a handsome young man with a square jaw, looked out at Charlie. "Are you Charlie?" Charlie nodded. "I'm here to take you to dinner with Rod Mandrake."

"Oh," Charlie said. "Okay."

The driver stepped out and opened the rear door for him. Charlie slid into the soft leather back seat and looked around. Magazines had been placed in the compartments on the seat backs before him. He chose one, a male skin magazine, and flipped through the pages until they had arrived at a large house built on a hill. Stilts supported a wide wooden deck and hot tub.

"Wow," Charlie whispered. He waited for the driver to open the car door, then walked up to the front of the cedar shingle house. Rod Mandrake himself answered the door with a smile.

"Charlie!" the director said. "Come in."

Rod gave Charlie a tour of the house, pointing out certain pieces of art that he enjoyed, then led him out to the deck. They sat in lounge chairs talking and drinking wine until a butler appeared and announced dinner.

"Come, Charlie," Rod said. "Let's go to the dining room."

Charlie found himself at one end of a long, gleaming table. There was one place setting, his, and a large, glowing candelabra. Sitting down, he looked up at Rod with a frown. "Aren't you eating?"

Rod nodded with a sly smile. "Oh yes, I'm going to eat. But, I like to eat a little differently than other people. You see, Charlie, I'm what people call a fetishist."

"A fetishist?" Charlie repeated.

"Yes. I have a somewhat unusual attraction to . . ." Rod paused and took a breath before saying quietly and with reverence, "Feet."

"Feet?"

"Yes, feet. Men's feet to be precise. I love men's feet." Rod pulled out the chair to Charlie's right and set it back against the wall. "Because of this fetish of mine, I have found that during dinner I am usually distracted by the very thought of my guest's feet. You know: the size, the shape, the taste, the smell. It was a few years back when I finally said to myself, 'Enough is enough.' I would be distracted no longer. Now when I entertain a young man in my home, I like to dine on the floor beneath the table with his feet on my plate."

Charlie glanced beneath the table and, sure enough, there was a place mat, a napkin, a plate, and a glass of water. He looked back up at Rod. "You want to eat your dinner off my feet?"

"Yes." Rod nodded and smiled. "Will that be a problem?"

Charlie tried to think about it logically. Would it be a problem? He had just clipped his toenails, thank God, so that wouldn't be an issue. He shrugged. "No, I guess not."

"Wonderful!" Rod turned and called out, "Robert! Please serve us." Rod then dropped to his hands and knees and crawled under the table. Charlie felt the director carefully untying his shoes and pulling them off. Rod then rolled Charlie's socks down his calves and off his feet.

"Oh, Charlie," Rod gasped. "You have marvelous feet. Has anyone ever told you that?"

Charlie shrugged, a little embarrassed, and said, "No, never. I've always thought they were too small."

"They're not too small, Charlie. Don't ever let anyone make you feel as if your feet are unworthy." Rod planted a soft kiss on each toe, bringing a giggle from Charlie, then reverently place his feet on the cool surface of what felt like a large dinner plate.

The butler, Robert, brought in two plates and placed one before Charlie then stooped and handed the other under the table to Rod. He turned and walked out of the room without a second glance. Charlie wondered how often he had served dinner in this fashion. The scrape of Rod's fork sounded just before Charlie felt the first of the food (mashed potatoes?) touch his feet. He almost jumped, but then held himself in check. More food followed and, as it was spread across or placed onto his feet, Charlie tried to match it up with what was on his plate. The gravy was warm and smooth, not too hot. A thoughtful cook.

"All right, Charlie," Rod's voice drifted up from beneath the table. "Let's begin."

"Okay." Charlie picked up his fork and knife and cut off a chunk of chicken. As he chewed his food, his curiosity overcame him and he peered under the table again. Rod was stretched out along the floor on his stomach, his hands clasped beneath his chest. His eyes were closed and his mouth was open, his tongue running slowly over the food spread across Charlie's feet. Rod's breast of chicken had been pre cut into bite size chunks, saving him from having to use the knife over Charlie's feet. As Charlie watched, Rod dipped his tongue down between two toes and licked up the potatoes and gravy that had slipped down there.

Charlie cocked his head and tried not to laugh as the food was consumed and Rod's tongue made its final laps around his feet. The meal was delicious, Charlie was full and happy, and the tongue bath that Rod was delivering beneath the table had actually gotten him surprisingly hard. Charlie did not mind a little foot worship now and then, but to have his date eat a meal off his feet was another thing entirely.

After finishing his food, Rod cleaned off Charlie's feet with his tongue and a napkin dipped in water. He crawled back out to stand next to Charlie and press the length of his erect cock against his shoulder.

"Feel like a little more fun?" Rod asked.

Charlie nodded, morbidly curious as to what other fetishes Rod had hidden away. He followed the director up a flight of stairs to a large room containing a king-sized bed with rubber sheets. A bathroom opened off the room as well, with a large, deep whirlpool tub and a shower stall. Obviously this was Rod's playroom.

The two men stripped, leaving their clothes neatly folded on a bench by the door. Rod took Charlie's hand and led him to the bed, stretching out on his back and pulling Charlie down on top of him. They kissed, their tongues mingling slowly as their hands roamed each other's bodies. Rod had a hairy body and Charlie found himself pulling his fingers through the mat of fur over and over again, as if he were stroking a pet.

Rolling over, Rod straddled Charlie's body and began moving his mouth down his torso. He sucked at Charlie's nipples, then moved lower to lick the length of his erection. Rod nuzzled his balls, licking at them as Charlie moaned and spread his legs. But he did not stop for long. He moved all the way down to Charlie's feet and began to slowly suck each toe, rubbing his fingers over the arches and kissing the bottoms.

Charlie closed his eyes and began to stroke himself. Rod opened his mouth and took all the toes on Charlie's right foot into his mouth, sucking and licking at the upper portion of his foot.

"Oh, Rod," Charlie groaned. "That feels really good."

Rod moaned around the foot in his mouth. He switched to Charlie's left foot and repeated the process, sucking all five toes at once. He massaged and licked the bottoms of Charlie's feet, then moved back up to begin sucking Charlie's cock. The man had a talented mouth, Charlie had to give him that. He knew how to work his tongue and lips.

Coming up for air, Rod grinned up at Charlie and said, "I want your foot in my ass."

Charlie blinked, then shrugged. "Okay." It wasn't high on his list of fantasies, but hell, if it would get Rod off it was fine by him.

Rod oiled himself up from a large pump container of lube, then reached down and lubed up Charlie's right foot. When he was done Rod lay on his back and pulled his legs up, raising his head to look down at Charlie. "Go ahead, put it in me."

Charlie reached out and slid a finger into Rod to loosen him up. The lube was slick, really slick, and soon Charlie had four fingers up inside the director's ass. Charlie pulled his fingers free then shifted position and rested his oiled up toes against Rod's gaping hole. He pressed forward and sank the top quarter of his foot up into Rod's asshole.

"Oh, yeah!" Rod groaned. "Get that foot up in me. Deeper!"

Charlie scooted forward and slid his foot deeper into the man. Rod groaned again and panted, "Now fuck me with it. Pump it in and out."

Charlie pulled his leg back and pushed it forward again, his toes withdrawing from Rod's sphincter then sliding back in. The oil glistened in the lights on the ceiling as Charlie picked up the pace. He watched in fascination as his foot fucked Rod's ass. It was pretty hot when he just did it without thinking about it.

"Oh, God, Charlie," Rod grunted. "I'm going to cum. I want to cum on your feet. Pull out."

Charlie pulled his foot out of Rod's ass and sat with his knees up and both feet planted on the rubber sheet. Rod struggled up to kneel before him and stroked himself to climax. Hot, thick wads of cum covered Charlie's feet, the warmth of the semen sinking between his toes.

"Oh, yeah," Rod gasped. "That was so hot. Oh, you have got a hot fucking pair of feet."

Charlie grinned. "Thanks."

Rod smiled, then leaned over to lick his cum off Charlie's feet. When he was done he sat up and said, "How would you like to cum?"

Charlie thought about it. "With your dick up my ass."

Rod nodded. "Sounds good. Suck me back up and I'll fuck your ass."

Charlie lay down on his back and sucked Rod's dick. It was long and thin, about seven and a half inches, with a tall head that looked to Charlie like the type of hat a marching bandleader might wear, or the guards in front of Buckingham Palace. He closed his eyes and swallowed the lengthening dick, holding it in his throat and massaging it with his tongue. Rod knelt on all fours above him and moaned as Charlie worked his tongue along the shaft.

"That feels really good," Rod said. "Keep working it like that. Oh yeah."

Charlie held it in his throat for a little longer, then began to work his way up the shaft to the tall head and back down the length again. Taking the member in his hand, he began to stroke it as he moved his mouth down to Rod's heavy, clean-shaven balls. He worked his tongue over the smooth sack and pulled them away from his groin one at a time, his lips fastened around the hard nut contained within. Rod grunted and moaned as Charlie worked his balls, then sighed when the fluffer moved back up to resume sucking his cock.

"Okay," Rod said and sat up, pulling his dick from Charlie's mouth. "Get your legs up."

Charlie raised his legs and felt Rod rub lube in his ass. He heard the tear of a condom package, and then Rod's palace guard of a cock was pressed up against the threshold of his ass. With a steady surge of pressure, Rod slid up into him. Charlie moaned and tried to get a grip on the rubber sheets, but the surface was slippery from the oil that had been used on his foot.

"Is that good?" Rod asked, buried to the bush inside him. He leaned down over Charlie's body and kissed him on the mouth.

"Oh, yeah. Get it up in me." Charlie grunted as Rod's hips began to pump. The man's cock arrowed into him, feeling as if it was driving deeper each time. Rod gripped Charlie's ankles, spreading his legs as he paused with his entire length embedded inside him. The director rotated his pelvis and wound his dick around Charlie's anal cavity. Charlie groaned and clenched his jaw.

"Oh, fuck!" he grunted. "Yeah, stuff that dick up in me and move it around. Oh, yeah. Spin it up inside me. Oh, God!"

Rod gyrated a few more times, then pulled back and began to batter at Charlie's stretched and eager hole once again. He ran his tongue over Charlie's feet, licking the soles and sucking on the toes as he plowed his dick between Charlie's jiggling ass cheeks.

Before too long, Charlie could feel his balls pull up and the inevitable tingle in his cock. He gasped as he stroked himself and raised his head, watching as Rod opened his mouth to take half of his right foot into his mouth.

"I'm going to cum," he panted.

"Mm hm." Rod's words were muffled around Charlie's foot before he removed it and plunged faster into him. "Shoot that hot load, baby," Rod directed. "All over your chest. Come on."

Charlie jerked himself to orgasm and felt his sphincter tighten around Rod's cock with each pulse of his balls. Cum splashed up over his chest and belly to mix with his sweat.

"Oh, man," Rod said. "I'm going to cum again." He continued to hammer at Charlie's hole until the head of his dick swelled and spewed his load into the tip of the condom. When he was through, Rod pulled slowly out of Charlie and lay next to him on the cool and slippery rubber sheet. "That was really hot."

Charlie smiled at him with a drowsy expression. "Yeah, it was."

"Would you like to take a shower?"

Charlie nodded and followed Rod into the bathroom. The shower stall was large with multiple showerheads aimed from all directions. They stepped in and cleaned up, soaping each other up and helping rinse off the lather. Afterwards, they had more wine on the deck and watched the sun go down behind the city.

Not long after that, Charlie left and rode in the Town Car back to his apartment building. The driver smiled at him as he stepped out of the car and Charlie considered inviting the handsome man up for a beer, but thought better of it. There would be other times. He nodded and gave the man a lingering look to let him know he was interested, but turned away and unlocked the door to his building.

The next morning, Charlie told Ken and Billy about his evening in hushed tones as they sat in the waiting room of the office. Ken nodded along with Charlie's story as if he had heard it all before.

"I'd heard rumors about Rod Mandrake, but never actually experienced his fetish before." Ken smiled and shook his head. "This city, I tell you."

Billy frowned at Charlie. "You fucked him with your foot?"

Charlie laughed and rubbed the younger man's head. "Yes, Billy. And maybe someday you'll get the chance to do the same thing."

Billy shook his head. "I dunno."

Kinitia stepped into the room and looked at them with a serious expression. Charlie caught her look and felt his heart jump. "Oh God, now what?"

She stepped forward, a folded piece of paper in her hands, and began to explain. "As a member of the adult video community I receive a list each year of all the nominees for the Golden Orifice Awards. These awards are given out to the adult movies which have demonstrated great creative insight or provided above and beyond entertainment."

"The Golden Orals?" Ken said with a gleam in his eye. "What are you saying, Kinitia?"

She regarded him for a moment, then turned to look at Charlie. "Along with these awards, there is a smaller but no less significant award that is handed out each year called The Hummer. This award recognizes achievement in the art of fluffing. We here at Fluffers, Inc. have never had a member of our team nominated for this award." She paused. "Until now."

Billy gasped and jumped up from the sofa. "Oh my God! Is it Charlie? Is it? It is, isn't it?"

Kinitia could contain herself no longer. A radiant smile lit her face and she nodded as her eyes sparkled down at Charlie's shocked face. "It's you, Farm Boy. You've been nominated to receive The Hummer!"

"Oh my God," Charlie said as the others danced and hugged around him. "Oh my God."

"Is that all you can say?" Ken cried. "This is a great thing! Not just for you, but for Kinitia's business! Once word of this gets out she'll have double the demand!"

They danced around some more and then Kinitia excused herself to go and make some phone calls. She reminded them that the awards ceremony was several weeks away and they all still had jobs to perform and not to let their notoriety go to their heads. She handed Charlie the letter on her way out of the room.

Charlie looked the letter over, finding his name listed along with four other men he had never heard of. Two were from Tongue In Cheeks, the company partly owned by Cedric, and the other two worked for a company called Oral Agreement. Scanning up along the list, Charlie found Rock Harding listed under Best Actor In a Gay Adult Movie and then noticed Cedric Wilmington listed under Best Director of a Gay Adult Movie. He groaned and shook his head. He would never be able to get away from Cedric Wilmington.

The hours flew by that day as they all reported to their assigned posts. Charlie had been assigned to another bear movie and was surprised to find a familiar face among the actors. A few weeks before, a strapping bear of a man had moved into the apartment across the hall, but Charlie had not had the chance to speak with him yet. And now here he was standing before Charlie with his cock hanging out of his boxer shorts.

"Uh, hi there," Charlie said. The man looked down at him and frowned. "I live across the hall from you."

Confusion crossed the man's dark features, then recognition flickered on. "Oh yeah. I've seen you around. How are you?"

Charlie shrugged and grabbed hold of the man's cock. "Good. I've seen you riding your bike. It's a nice one."

The man nodded and smiled. "Thanks. I like to go out on the trails. I'm Brent Harrington."

"Charlie Heggensford." They shook hands, then Charlie continued to stroke the man. "I like your goatee."

Brent reached up to stroke the thick, dark goatee around his mouth. "You do? I was thinking of shaving it off."

"Don't do it. It looks good. It suits you." Charlie opened his mouth and leaned forward to start sucking Brent's cock.

"That feels nice, Charlie," Brent said. He pulled his T-shirt over his head and rubbed his hands over his hairy belly. "You're a good fluffer."

"Thanks," Charlie said around his mouthful of dick. He sucked slow and long, bringing Brent up to full arousal until he was needed on the set. "Good luck."

"Thanks for the fluffing," Brent said. "Maybe we can get together back at the building sometime."

Charlie nodded noncommittally. "Maybe."

Brent walked off, dropping his boxer shorts as he headed for the king sized bed brightly illuminated by hot studio lights. The man stretched out beside his partner, a big red headed bear of a man with a full beard and a slightly larger belly than Brent's. The director called for quiet, then said, "Action!" and Brent delivered a few lines as his acting partner reached over and tweaked his nipples. Brent leaned down and took the red head's solid, seven-inch dick into his mouth.

As he sucked the red head's cock, Brent got to his hands and knees and his partner reached out to tug slowly at Brent's dick. The man soon slid over and began to suck Brent's cock as he moved a hand back and started to finger Brent's fur shrouded asshole.

Before long Brent was lying at the edge of the bed with his legs in the air and the red head was slamming his dick up Brent's ass. Brent grunted with each thrust and egged his partner on, clenching his teeth and reaching out to rub his hands over the man's belly.

"Yeah!" Brent snarled. "Poke that ass! Fuck it! Get your dick in me."

The director called for a break and the red head reluctantly pulled out of Brent's ass. He stripped off the condom and both men turned their heads to look for Charlie. The director looked around as well and finally called out, "Where's the fucking fluffer?"

Charlie jumped up from the crate he had been sitting on, his mind a million miles away, and rushed up to the set as the cameramen changed angles and the lights were moved.

"Come on, fluffer," the red head said in a high pitched, whiny voice that stopped Charlie in his tracks. It was such an odd voice to come from that large of a man. "I'm losing my boner."

Charlie smiled and knelt before both men, the red head standing by the bed with his pelvis cocked and one hand resting on a fleshy hip. Brent lay stretched out along the bed with his legs hanging over the side. He had a small, satisfied smile on his face. Charlie reached up and began stroking the red head as he leaned forward and took Brent's slowly deflating dick in his mouth. The big, hairy man sighed and raised his head slightly to smile down at Charlie.

"Thanks, Charlie," Brent said. "I needed that."

"Yeah, and I do, too," the red head whined and Charlie turned his attention to the man's wilting penis. As he sucked the man's dick back to its previous hardness, Charlie bumped his forehead up against the man's firm, hair covered belly with each down stroke. He wondered idly if he might get a bruise on his forehead from the impact.

"Okay," the director called out. "Dry them off and see if they need more makeup. Fluffer, keep sucking until we're ready to go."

Charlie continued moving back and forth between the hairy men as assistants dabbed at the sweaty men with towels. A make up man approached, a large, butch bear who possessed a surprisingly light touch with the applicators, and he brushed at them until they were ready to go.

"Okay, fluffer be gone," the director called with a wave of his hand. Charlie released the red head's cock and moved out of the line of the hot lights. Turning, he watched as the red head applied a fresh condom and lubed it up. Brent shifted position on the bed, getting to his hands and knees and angling his body at the corner of the mattress. The red head approached him and the cameras started rolling as he slipped into Brent's glistening hole.

As the scene continued, Charlie looked around the set of the movie, his mind whirling from the day's events. Nominated for an award in his first year in California. He poked through the props for the movie: dildos, butt plugs, lots of lube, some military boots, and a leather mask with zippers. Charlie looked around, then held the mask up and checked above the eye zippers for any sign of eyebrows. Nothing. He returned the mask and went back to his chair, his mind working through the possibilities of who might have broken into Kinitia's office and why.

A new full figured hairy man appeared before him and presented his soft penis. Charlie opened up and began to service the man, his tongue curling around the shaft and dipping occasionally into the piss slit. The bear grunted with each suck and tried to begin humping his face, but Charlie backed away from the cock and began to suck the man's balls instead, keeping him erect with his fist until he too was called to the set.

Brent walked past Charlie on his way to the shower. He was covered with sweat and dried cum. His goatee looked like it had taken the full brunt of his partner's load: globs of drying cum clung to the whiskers as he smiled at Charlie.

"It went well?" Charlie asked.

Brent waggled his dick at Charlie and grinned. "It always goes well with me."

As Brent entered the trailer, Charlie sat in his chair and took a deep breath. Maybe things would be all right after all. Maybe life was evening out and good things were going to start happening. Maybe it was the start of a new way of life in LA.

9

Chip Off the Old Tinitia

One day shortly after his nomination, Charlie was sitting in the waiting area of Fluffers, Inc. with Billy watching *Innerspace* when Kinitia's voice crackled over the intercom, calling him up front. Charlie stood up but waited until Dennis Quaid's bare ass flashed across the screen before turning with a contented sigh and walking up the hall. Kinitia and Ken were sitting at the front desk with the schedule book open before them.

"Hi guys," Charlie said. "What's up?"

Kinitia raised her head and smiled at him. "How are your throat muscles feeling, Farm Boy?"

Charlie shrugged. "Fine. Why do you ask?"

"I need someone to take a little trip with me," Kinitia said and tossed a stray extension over her shoulder. "It's a very important trip that will require self control and a lot of manners. That's why I'm thinking of you for it."

Charlie smirked. Wouldn't his mother be proud that all those years of her teaching him to be polite were finally being recognized. "Okay. What's the story with the trip?"

Kinitia took a breath, then explained. "I received a call last night from someone very important. This person requested my help in finding a fluffer who would help in the quick creation of a gay porn movie."

Charlie narrowed his eyes with suspicion. "It's not Cedric, is it?"

Kinitia smiled and exchanged an amused look with Ken. "No, it's not Cedric Wilmington."

"Okay then," Charlie said with a frown. "Who is it?"

"My grandmother," Kinitia replied. "Tinitia Jones."

Charlie felt his mouth drop open. "Your grandmother is directing a gay porno?"

Kinitia nodded with a calm smile. "She has become bored in her retirement and wants to do something a little more creative. I guess she has this hairdresser down there who knows a bunch of hot guys who have been talking about acting in gay porn for a while. So, my grandmother and her hairdresser came up with a story line, pitched it to these guys and they all bought in." Kinitia shrugged. "Easy as pie, she said."

Ken said with a smirk, "Sort of a hardcore version of "The Little Rascals" when you think about it. You know, 'Hey, everyone, let's put on a show!'"

Charlie and Kinitia laughed, then Charlie asked, "Is it just me going with you?"

"Yes. You and I will drive down to San Diego tomorrow morning. We'll be staying overnight, so pack a bag. Ken will run the shop while we're gone." Kinitia took a breath and said. "What do you think?"

Charlie nodded. "Sounds good. Let's do it. I'm looking forward to meeting your grandmother."

"Great. I'll call Grammy and tell her the good news." Kinitia picked up the phone and Charlie headed back to the waiting room to continue watching the movie, curiosity about Kinitia's grandmother burning within him. What would Tinitia be like? Strong and harsh, or grandmotherly with warm cookies and milk? And how would he feel sucking cock in front of a grandmother? He shook his head and tried to clear his mind. All his questions would be answered tomorrow.

The next morning they left early to beat the traffic. As they drove along in silence, Charlie realized how little he knew of

Kinitia's background. He cleared his throat, smiled over at her, and asked tentatively, "So, you were raised by your grandmother?"

Kinitia smirked, but replied. "That's right. My mom ran off when I was five. She started seeing Quentin again, the guy who used to own the club, and then just left one night."

"Wow, that must have been tough."

Kinitia shrugged. "No different than how it had been. She was kind of an absentee mother. Grammy raised me even when she was still living with us."

"So how did you get into this business?" Charlie asked. "Did you end up dancing at the bar?"

Kinitia gave him an incredulous look. "Dance? For those pigs who came in there every night? Not on your life, Farm Boy. I helped out behind the bar and backstage. And I learned a lot about dancing from Grammy during rehearsals. But she would never let me get up on that stage. She wanted something better for her granddaughter, and I'm very grateful for that."

Charlie nodded, then asked, "But how did you get involved in the business?"

Kinitia grinned at him. "You mean the fluffer business?" She shook her head. "You still have trouble with that, don't you?"

Charlie shrugged and blushed. "It's just so frank and blatant ... I'm not used to it. Things are a little different back in Idaho. Not much, but enough."

"I bet they are," Kinitia replied. "Okay, you want the history of Kinitia Jones? Here it is. When I was sixteen I started working as bartender at the club. Grammy let me do that because I had a bar between me and the customers. She was very protective. I didn't date much in high school. I didn't want anybody to know my grandmother ran a strip club, you know?" Charlie nodded understandingly. "So after I graduated, I went to college during the day and worked the bar at night. I can make any drink under the sun, but mostly I just poured draft beers. A waste of talent, if you ask me. Well, one night this fine looking gentleman walked in and I was blown away. He was gorgeous. Muscular and handsome and oh, so smooth. Turned out he was a porn star. A gay porn star. His name was Tyrone Biggun."

Charlie laughed. "Nice name."

Kinitia nodded. "He carried it well, if you know what I mean. Anyway, he was in the club that night visiting his sister who was a waitress and while she was serving drinks he sat at the bar and we talked and talked for hours. He came back at least three times a week after that and we got to be good friends. Sometimes he took me to the sets where he worked and I noticed how the director would have crewmembers fluff the stars, but then the lights would need to be set up and the actors would go down and it was a continuous battle. Sometimes the stars would bring in their boyfriends or tricks to blow them, but then that usually led to some jealous tantrums on the set or rampant drug use and the actors were no use if they were too coked up or stoned. That's when I came up with the idea of a fluffer dispatch service."

"And Fluffers, Inc. was born, huh?" Charlie said.

"Not right away. I wanted to finish my degree first and I didn't know the first thing about the porn industry. So I started to network. I used Tyrone's contacts to meet other people and I started pitching my idea. And one of the crewmembers I talked with during that time was a young, ambitious man named Cedric Wilmington."

Charlie's mouth dropped open. "Cedric was just a crewmember?"

Kinitia laughed. "We all have to start somewhere, Farm Boy. Anyway, I think I took too long to get the ball rolling. Plus I was nervous about starting my own business and procrastinated. But about a year later I applied for a business license and found out another fluffer dispatch service was in the works named Tongue In Cheeks, and listed as one of the owners was none other than--"

"Cedric Wilmington!" Charlie finished. "That sneaky bitch. He stole your idea. I don't believe it!"

Kinitia shook her head. "I was surprised at first, too. But after all these years I understand the nasty old cow a little better. He's just a small-minded bitch. But enough about Cedric. I squared my shoulders, let his idea theft go, and took some money from Grammy as start up capital. I found the office, hired a few people, including Ken Carlton, and we started advertising in the porn industry papers. Before too long we were getting calls. It was easier for a director to schedule someone professional, clean, and prompt to provide fluffer service than it was to pull in some trash from the street and give him $20. I opened the doors seven years ago and we've been going strong ever since."

"Wow," Charlie said. "That's amazing. Quite a story."

Kinitia nodded. "It's been an interesting ride."

"What happened to Tyrone? Are you two still friends?"

Kinitia's face grew sad and she shook her head. "He died of an overdose."

"Oh." Charlie shifted in his seat. "Sorry. That's too bad."

"Yeah, it is," Kinitia said quietly. "He was a good person. Just got mixed up in some bad shit." She turned to Charlie and said sternly, "So keep that shit out of your system, Farm Boy. Got it?"

"Don't worry," Charlie replied. "I'm clean and expect to stay that way."

"You'd better. If I think anyone on my staff has a problem I'll slap them in rehab faster than they can snort up a line." She nodded to herself, her jaw set, and Charlie could tell Tyrone's death had had quite an impact on her life.

They fell silent, Charlie having run out of questions and Kinitia thinking back over her memories. Charlie slipped into a light doze as Kinitia hummed along with a CD of Chinese meditation music.

Some time later, the car slowed on an exit ramp and Charlie blinked awake to peer around with bleary eyes. They were in a pleasant neighborhood with tree-lined streets and well manicured lawns. Charlie looked around with interest as the suburb gave way to another gathering of well-tended houses and established trees. Kinitia drove along several roads and then turned into a long asphalt driveway that curved through lush grounds up to a group of Victorian style condominiums gathered around a pond with a fountain spouting up from the middle. Ducks and geese floated lazily at the edge of the water. All the Victorian fronts were painted with different colors and Kinitia pulled to a stop before one painted yellow, purple, orange, and red.

"Wow," Charlie said quietly. "This is really nice."

Kinitia lowered her head to look up along the condominium before her. "Yep. Grammy retired in style, let me tell you. She raised her family in a small, two bedroom house south of LA and vowed to never have less than three bedrooms ever again."

"You were raised in south central LA?" Charlie asked in awe. He had seen plenty of movies on cable back home and had long harbored a belief that South Central LA was one of the most dangerous areas in the country.

Kinitia blushed and looked away. "Not really. We were raised south of LA." She hesitated. "In Anaheim."

"Anaheim?" Charlie echoed, and then narrowed his eyes. "Isn't that where Disneyland is located?"

"Yeah, I know, I know," Kinitia said and waved her hand in dismissal as she opened her car door. "Magic Kingdom and all that shit. But let me tell you, the traffic alone from that place is enough to make anyone go postal."

They stepped out and Charlie walked to the trunk.

"So how many bedrooms does she have in this condo?" Charlie asked as he pulled their bags from the trunk.

"Six." Kinitia replied and Charlie stared at her in surprise.

"Six?"

Kinitia shrugged. "She has a lot of stuff."

The bright purple door opened at the top of a set of concrete steps and a solidly built black woman stepped out on the porch. She threw her arms open and cried, "Kinny!"

"Hi Grammy!" Kinitia said and dashed excitedly up the stairs to hug her grandmother tight.

Charlie took a moment to assess Tinitia as the women hugged and rocked on the porch. She had bright orange hair swept back into a tight bun, a soft, young looking face and a thick, stocky body with wide, solid hips and shoulders. She wore a white, flower print dress and a pair of half glasses on a chain around her neck that swayed as she rocked her granddaughter. Tinitia released Kinitia and turned her head to peer down the steps at Charlie.

"Is that the new fluffer you've been telling me about?" Tinitia raised the glasses to her nose and lifted her chin to look at Charlie through the lenses. "Oh, my. He does look very innocent, doesn't he?"

Kinitia laughed. "Come here, Charlie. This is my grandmother, Tinitia Jones. Grammy, this is Charlie Heggensford."

Charlie ascended the steps and extended his hand with a smile. "Hello, Mrs. Jones, it's a great honor to meet you. I've heard a lot about you from Kinitia."

Tinitia and Kinitia looked at one another from the corners of their eyes, then both burst into laughter. Charlie stood before them with his hand still out and a confused look on his face as the women laughed.

"Well, isn't that the shit?" Tinitia finally said. "Come here, boy, and let me give you a proper greeting." She pulled him into her strong arms and hugged him tight. "Welcome to San Diego. Are you ready to suck your way through some monster dicks?"

Charlie felt his face flush and found he could only nod. He followed the laughing women into the house and stopped in the living room. The room was decorated in Early American furniture with paintings of Colonial life hanging on the walls. A ceramic log was burning in the gas fireplace and a small kettle hung over the fire.

"Your bedroom is upstairs, Charlie," Tinitia called. "First room on the left. And Kinitia's is right across the hall. Your room is called Tomorrowland and Kinitia's is Victorian England."

Charlie went upstairs and leaned into the first room on the left. It contained modern furniture with an art deco feel, like the futuristic sets from a 1960s movie. The bed was smooth silver laminate and the furniture was all rounded edges and white plastic. Charlie dropped his bag by the bed and crossed the hall. This room was decorated with heavy velvet drapes, flowered wallpaper, and dark wooden furniture. The bed was a four poster canopy with sheer curtains. Ornate picture frames displayed photos of Kinitia through the years and he took a moment to look at them.

He joined the women in the living room and found tea and cookies waiting. While Kinitia discussed business matters with Tinitia, Charlie amused himself by glancing into the rooms on the first level. The kitchen was decorated in a 1950s American motif complete with older appliances that sparkled like new. The bathroom down the hall was done up like something out of King Arthur's Court and the main bedroom at the end of the hall sported Ancient Chinese tapestries and rice paper drawings. Obviously Tinitia had spent some time absorbing the vibes given off by Disneyland.

A knock at the front door drew him back to the living room where he found a large, overweight black man laughing heartily as he hugged Kinitia. The man was tall, at least six foot five, and had to weigh about 350 pounds. His massive arms were wrapped around Kinitia's shoulders and his shaved head gleamed in the light coming in from the windows overlooking the pond.

"Kinitia, it is so good to see you!" the man rumbled in a deep voice. He opened his eyes and spotted Charlie hovering in the hallway. "Oh, my. And who is this delicious little lump of confection?" The man released Kinitia and lumbered gracefully across the room to loom over Charlie and present his hand. "Allow me to introduce myself. I am Waldo Wallace. And who might you be?"

Charlie flinched as his fingers were swallowed up by Waldo's huge hand. "Um, Charlie Heggensford, sir. Nice to meet you."

Waldo looked back at Kinitia and gave her a look. "Such manners, Ms. Jones. You do find the pretty ones, don't you?"

"All right, Waldo," Kinitia said. "Stop accosting my employee and let's get this show on the road."

"Well, Charlie," Waldo replied with a bright smile. "It is definitely nice to meet you." Waldo turned and headed for the front door. "Come along, Jones women. You too, Charles."

As Charlie and Kinitia walked out the door, she leaned over and said to him, "Waldo is Grammy's hair dresser. She's been going to him for over twenty years. He's the one who helped her find these actors and come up with the story line for the movie."

"He seems very nice."

"Oh, he is. And he's just like every other man I've met: horny as the day is long." Kinitia shook her head and opened her car door. "I just don't know where they found a place to film this movie." She stopped and frowned as Waldo and Tinitia walked past his

Audi TT Roadster and headed off along a path around the pond. "Hey, Grammy!" she called. "Where you headed?"

"Come on, Ms. Jones," Waldo said over his shoulder. "It's not that far."

Kinitia and Charlie shrugged to one another and followed the two along the path until they came to the activities center for the condominium group. Waldo produced a key and unlocked a door then held it open for the rest of them. They entered a large, banquet style hall complete with bar, serving kitchen, and several round tables set up with tablecloths and artificial flower arrangements.

"Very nice, Waldo," Kinitia said, then shook her head and asked, "I don't get it. Are we crashing a wedding?"

"No, honey," Waldo exclaimed. "We're filming a movie! It's a wedding motif. Sort of. Any way, it's a wedding reception type of setting and then all hell breaks loose. We'll make the other shit up as we go along."

Tinitia nodded and clapped her hands together. "Bring on the dicks! Where are those pretty little bastards you lined up for me last week, Waldo? I need another look at 'em!"

Waldo laughed and pulled out his cell phone. "I'm sure they just got lost trying to get here. There was a big rave going on last night down by the docks and they probably haven't slept since night before last. I'll call Dwond right now." He stepped away to make his phone call and Kinitia turned to her grandmother.

"Grammy, I don't know about this," she said quietly. "I don't think the condo association would appreciate having their activities building used to film a gay porn video."

Tinitia made a face and waved Kinitia's concern away. "Ah, you young people. Where's your guts? Everyone told me I couldn't run a strip joint all those years ago too, and look what I did. Ran that shit hole like nobody's business and made more money than all your ancestors combined." She gave a single, curt nod, putting an end to the discussion. "We'll be fine. I'm going over here to check out the camera equipment."

While Waldo made his calls and Tinitia tinkered with a couple of VHS cameras standing on tripods in a corner, Kinitia and Charlie found some extra tablecloths and taped them up over the windows.

As they approached a sliding door leading out to a shuffleboard and patio set they found several elderly people, men and women, peering curiously into the room. They both jumped, glanced at one another, then taped up the tablecloth, effectively blocking out all views from the outside. As they hung the final tablecloth, the door banged open and seven large, well muscled black men stepped into the banquet hall. Charlie surveyed their dark, gleaming flesh beneath tank tops and half shirts and felt himself grow hard. Each of the men carried himself with such a self-assured, sexual stance Charlie could not help staring. Several of the men stared back and winked, grinning as their eyes swept up and down his body.

"Well," Tinitia snapped and at the tone of her voice the seven men quickly straightened up. "It's about damn time you all moseyed on in here. Get into the bathroom and change your damn clothes. There're tuxedoes in there that will fit each of you. And no fucking around and no drugs! Got it? First one I hear sniffing like they've got hay fever I'll toss him out on his ass. Now, get along!"

The seven men jumped and filed into the bathroom. There was a loud commotion as they all tried to change at once and soon they began to appear one by one, adjusting bow ties and cummerbunds. Charlie went to assist them and found he could only smile and blush at the men as they talked to him in low, enticing voices.

"All right then!" Tinitia shouted. "Listen up! I want Dwond and Gerard up over here to film some scenes."

The two men stepped forward and Waldo reviewed their lines, then started filming. Charlie sat on the floor against the wall and watched with interest. Tinitia was an impressive dictator of a director. She was out to make a gay porn video and by God no one was going to stop her. Charlie could see where Kinitia learned to be strong.

Before long Dwond and Gerard were kissing and fondling one another by the bar as Terrell hovered in the background acting as bartender and watching. Tinitia got them to strip each other down and then walked Dwond through lifting Gerard up onto the bar on his belly and spreading his ass open to begin feasting on his dark, hairless pucker.

"That's it, baby," Tinitia called out. "Get your tongue up inside him. Uh huh. Work it up in there. Gerard, I want to see your face. Show me you like it. Kinitia, you get his expressions on film, now. Don't fuck this up, baby."

Kinitia and Waldo moved the cameras around and tried to stay out of each other's way. Before too long, Tinitia called out, "Cut! Good! Now, let's get ready for the fucking scene. Waldo, we need to move some lights around." Tinitia swiveled her head and screeched, "Fluffer! Keep them up!"

Charlie leaped up and crossed to the bar. He knelt before Dwond and, smiling up at the handsome face beaming down, leaned in to begin sucking the long, thick cock. The man's dick was very thick at the base, so thick Charlie's fingers could not connect as he gripped it tight. And he was long, at least eight inches, with a fat pink head glistening with pre cum.

Gerard slid down off the bar and turned to present his own thick prick for servicing. Charlie pulled both men's balls down away from their groins and switched his attention back and forth between them, sucking first one then the other. Gerard was uncut and slightly longer than Dwond, Charlie guessed eight and a half inches as he wrapped his lips around the shaft and peeled back the foreskin with his sheathed teeth to run his tongue over the smooth head.

"Okay! We're ready!" Tinitia shouted and Charlie moved away, wiping the spit from his chin. "And ... action!"

Dwond flipped Gerard over onto his back and began eating his ass and sucking his balls. He was into the scene, closing his eyes and grunting as Gerard bumped his hips up and down to run his asshole over Dwond's lips and tongue. Dwond then pulled Gerard off the bar and turned him around, positioning him just so as he stroked some lube along his condom covered dick, then burrowed into the man with a single thrust.

"Oh yeah!" Gerard cried out and closed his eyes as he thrust his hips back and impaled himself as much as possible. "Sink that big dick in me. Oh, fuck!"

"Good!" Tinitia called out. "Get it up inside him and then ride the hell out of his ass, baby!"

Charlie blinked and tried not to think of Tinitia as a grandmother as he watched her direct the scene. She knew all the right words and what to say to get her actors to perform, that was for sure. He wondered where she had picked it up.

"Okay!" Tinitia turned to look at them. "I need two more up and ready to go. They're going to just join right in, so Charlie get your mouth to work over there. I need Gordon and Collin in ten minutes!"

Charlie got to his knees as the two men approached him and he reached out to unzip their tuxedo pants. Looking up, he smiled pleasantly at each one.

"How are you?" he asked politely.

"Ready to spray a big old load," Collin replied with a grin. "Can you help me out with that?"

Charlie blushed. "I can get you ready for that." He fished Collin's thick cock and low hanging balls from inside his pants, then pulled out Gordon's dick and balls and mentally compared the two. They seemed to be exactly the same length and shape.

"People think we're brothers," Gordon replied. "We do a lot of group sex."

"Oh. Well. I'm sure the brother thing would work in certain circles," Charlie replied.

Gordon shrugged. "It does."

Charlie began sucking first Collin and then Gordon, taking each man deep into his throat and running his tongue along the shaft. When he released one from his mouth he began to immediately stroke it, keeping it hard in his tight fist. He also occasionally dropped his tongue down to each man's low hanging balls, licking and sucking at them as he stroked their cocks.

Collin and Gordon were called away and Tinitia shouted out for Terrell to move out from behind the bar and out of the picture. Gordon and Collin walked up and Collin rolled a condom onto his long, dark prick and, leaving his pants on as he pulled off his shirt to expose his smooth, muscular chest, bent Dwond forward over Gerard's back and slid deep inside him with one stroke.

Gordon presented his own hardened cock to Gerard and the man began to suck it as Dwond continued to pump into his ass and Collin started to fuck Dwond.

"Good!" Tinitia shouted. "I like it! Keep up the rhythm! Show me good length, babies. I need to see more cock pulling out and pushing in. Nice. Very nice. Keep it up. Kinitia, stay on Gerard and Gordon. Waldo, move between Collin and Dwond."

The scene ended as Dwond shot his load first, spattering across Gerard's sweaty back while Collin continued to fuck his ass. Gordon came next, spraying his thick, white load over Gerard's face and shoulders and using his softening dick to smear the semen around. Collin came next and practically covered Dwond's back with his load, semen arching high into the air and hitting Dwond on the back of the neck and shoulders. Gerard straightened up and Dwond slipped two fingers up his asshole, banging them furiously up into him as he stroked himself to climax over Gordon's flat stomach and black tuxedo pants.

"Damn," Waldo hissed as he filmed the cum shot. "We'll have to clean those before we take them back."

Charlie began fluffing Terrell, Tyler, and Samson as the other four men went into the bathroom to clean up. The next scene was being shot in the kitchen and Waldo rolled up a wooden door that exposed a serving counter and a large wooden butcher block behind. As the lights were set up, Charlie began sucking Terrell, seven and a half inches and thick as his grip at the base, then moved to Tyler who was eight and half inches and as thick as his grip at the base. When both men were well on their way to full erection, he turned to begin working on Samson and stopped to stare.

The man's cock was hanging out of the zipper of his pants and had to be at least seven inches long, soft. His balls dangled behind his penis and fell halfway to his knees. Charlie looked up and found Samson grinning down at him. A gold tooth gleamed in the corner of his mouth and his shaved head glowed in the lights.

"Think you can handle it, fluffer?" Samson rumbled in a deep voice.

"I can try," Charlie replied and closed his eyes. He took the monster dick down into his throat and felt himself gag. If this was how long Samson was soft, what would he be like when he was hard? He pulled back and had Samson move over so he was between Tyler and Terrell. Using his hands on the other two men, Charlie began to suck for all he was worth on Samson's mutant dick. The cock grew and expanded in his mouth, filling his throat as it hardened.

Backing off, Charlie moved between the other two men, sucking and slurping along their cocks as he stroked Samson with both hands. The man was at full mast and had to be eleven inches long. He was as big around as a beer can and Charlie marveled at the size of the thing.

"Okay, let's go!" Tinitia called out. "If we finish up the sex scenes today we can get the rest of the scenes tomorrow. I need Terrell and Tyler. Charlie, keep Samson hard until he's needed!"

Charlie watched the other two men walk off and then went to town on Samson's monstrous cock. The thing was a work of art. It was enormous. Where in the world would he stick it? Charlie winced as he considered the effects of taking that dick up his ass. Would it even fit half way?

Tyler and Terrell were engaged in a 69 on the butcher block counter, each man sucking greedily on the other's dick as they slipped fingers deep into one another's assholes. Waldo and Kinitia worked to capture it all on film as Charlie kept trying to take all of Samson down his throat at once.

"Okay now," Tinitia called. "I need my big boy. Where's Samson?"

The man pulled slowly out of Charlie's mouth and reached down to chuck him under the chin. "Nice job, fluffer. Most guys puke on me when they try to take me as deep as you did."

Charlie smiled at him and tried not to think about just how close to puking he had come a couple of times. He watched Samson walk into the scene and lean down to start licking Terrell's asshole as he pulled on his massive cock. Terrell groaned around his mouthful of Tyler's balls and then eased himself up off the butcher block and presented his ass to Samson. Tyler stretched out on the butcher block on his back and Terrell began to suck his dick as Samson unwound an extra large condom along the length of his cock.

Using a liberal amount of lube, Samson slipped a finger into Terrell, then two. Soon he had four fingers bumping up into Terrell's stretched and glistening hole. He pulled his hand free and moved up to pressed the thick bulb of his circumcised head against the opening of Terrell's ass and pressed steadily up into the man. He got halfway inside Terrell before he backed out and tried again. It took five times before Terrell's rectal muscles relaxed enough to admit the length of Samson's dick, and even then he screwed up his face at the end of each thrust.

Charlie knelt in amazement and watched the scene before him. He had never seen a dick that big before. Movement to his right pulled his attention back and he found the four men from the previous scene ready to be sucked back to erection for their next scenes. He began to blow each man in turn and closed his eyes as he fell into a rhythm. He would suck one, stroke two others, then move on to the next cock and start sucking as he shifted his hands to stroke two different dicks.

As he moved along, a fifth cock was added to the line up that Charlie did not notice. He simply reached out a hand with his eyes closed and found the limp penis hanging there. He kept his eyes shut, figuring that Tyler or Terrell was done with their scene and needed fluffing as he pulled gently on the organ. A few minutes later he opened his mouth and took the soft, wrinkled penis into his mouth. He sucked and sucked on it, but it wouldn't budge. There seemed to be no blood flowing to the organ.

Charlie frowned around the dick in his mouth and increased his suction. Still the withered dick did not harden. It didn't even twitch. Opening his eyes, Charlie looked up at the dick's owner and found an elderly black man standing before him. The man's eyes were shut and his mouth hung open in a broad smile. His dentures were riding up off his gums, almost ready to fall out and land on Charlie's face.

Charlie spit the dick out of his mouth and backed up. The four men standing before him turned to assess the new arrival with furrowed brows. None of them had noticed him enter the room.

"Who the fuck is that?" Dwond asked from the opposite end of the line.

"Good fucking question," Charlie snapped and stood up. He sniffed his hands and groaned. "Oh, for God's sake! I smell like Ben Gay!"

Tinitia turned around at the commotion and walked up. "What the fuck is going on here?" She saw the elderly man still standing with his eyes closed, his mouth open and his shriveled penis hanging out and threw her hands up in the air. "Oh, for the love of Pete! Harmond! Harmond, you old fool!"

She reached out and poked the man in the chest, almost knocking him backwards. His eyes fluttered open behind his thick glasses and he smiled at her as he slipped his dentures back into place. "Hi, Tinitia! Great party!"

"Get out of here, you old buzzard!" Tinitia snapped.

"What?" Harmond replied. "Can't hear you. This is my bad ear." He turned his head. "Talk into this one."

"I said," Tinitia repeated, leaning in and raising her voice. "This is a private party! Get out!"

"Oh! Well, guess I'll be going then." Harmond looked at Charlie and winked. "Best blow job I've had in five years."

"You damn fool," Tinitia muttered. "That's the first blow job you've had in twenty years."

Harmond turned and walked stiffly to the door, his penis still hanging out of his baggy trousers. Charlie looked at Tinitia and said, "Shouldn't we tell him he's hanging out?"

Tinitia waved her hand at Harmond's back as he pushed through the door. "Nah, let him be. It'll give Maple and Harriet a thrill as he passes by their condo. Charlie, go lock the door so no more lookie loos can wander in."

She went back to directing the scene and Charlie twisted the thumb lock on the door. He then headed into the bathroom and tried to wash the smell of Ben Gay off his hands and face. Unfortunately, he was to discover that Ben Gay is a stubborn odor and it would be days before he could no longer smell a trace of it on himself.

The scene between Terrell, Samson, and Tyler was just coming to its climax as Charlie emerged from the bathroom. Samson picked up the pace of his driving dock pile, spearing into Terrell's amazingly accommodating asshole with force until he pulled out and stripped the condom off to pump a drenching load of semen over Terrell's lower back and ass cheeks. Tyler came next, pulling his dick from Terrell's mouth and stroking himself to climax over Terrell's shoulder and neck. Terrell straightened up and leaned back against Samson as he jerked off onto Tyler's softened cock, balls, and thighs.

"Great!" Tinitia cried out. "I love it! Okay, we're moving on to the next scene! Charlie, keep those other four up and ready to go."

Later that evening Charlie, Tinitia, and Kinitia walked tiredly around the duck pond to Tinitia's door. The actors and Waldo had all gone out for drinks and Charlie had declined the offer to go with them. His jaw and throat were sore from hours of fluffing and all he wanted to do was crawl into his futuristic bed and go to sleep.

"Charlie," Tinitia said to him as he headed up the stairs inside the condo, "You did good today. You're a good worker and I like that about a man. Do you have a fella?"

Charlie thought fleetingly of Rock Harding and shook his head. "No, ma'am."

Tinitia nodded. "Keep it that way. Men are trouble. They are the devil incarnate and you're better off without one. Buy yourself a good dildo and a lot of movies and you'll be happy for life."

Charlie smiled. "I'll keep that in mind."

Tinitia glanced along the hallway to see if Kinitia was out of the King Arthur bathroom yet. The door was still closed and she lowered her voice to say, "I've got a few dildos in my room down the hall here. If you want, I could loan you one on a trial basis. Kind of like a test drive."

Charlie tried not to make a disgusted face as the mental image of Tinitia satisfying herself with a dildo flashed across his mind. "Uh, well, thanks, ma'am. That's awful kind of you. But I've got a few of my own back home."

Tinitia nodded and gave him a thumbs up. "Good for you. But remember: if you need a new one, let me know. I've got a connection that'll get 'em for me cheap."

Charlie smiled and gave her a weak thumbs up in return. "I'll remember that. G'night." He turned to head upstairs and held off shivering until he was safely in his room behind a locked door.

Stripping off his clothes and stretching out on the bed, he pulled on his rapidly hardening cock, bringing the blood surging back into the organ. He had had an erection for the last few hours while fluffing the actors and it felt like his balls were going to explode. He closed his eyes and brought to mind Samson's massive dick, how it felt and tasted in his mouth and how it had looked spearing into Terrell's asshole. Charlie remembered the sight of Terrell's sphincter stretched almost paper thin as it had expanded to allow Samson entry. How would that big, thick cock feel pummeling up into his own asshole?

As if in response Charlie felt his sphincter tighten and release, his prostate twitching as if in anticipation of an invasion by the mutant prick. The head had been smooth and bulbous, forging a blunt end that would spread his rectal muscles wide before it. Charlie could almost feel Samson's log of a cock burrowing into him, plundering his ass and leaving it glistening and gaping when it was through.

With a grunt, Charlie covered his chest and belly with a tremendous load of semen. The thick, sticky fluid burst from his cock with more force than he had managed in a long time. He stroked himself to completion and lay there panting, his mind drifting as the cum dried on his skin.

He fell asleep sprawled out on his back and did not wake up until the sounds of Tinitia making breakfast in her retro kitchen brought him around the following morning. He got up, groggy and crusty with dried cum, and pulled on his jeans to shuffle down the hall to the 1920s style bathroom. Peering through slitted eyes at the gaudy wallpaper and antique fittings he decided he was going to be happy to get back home that evening.

10

Word Of Mouth

Charlie found that he was quite the mini celebrity following his nomination for The Hummer award. Actors lined up before him while he worked, each interested in experiencing the sensation of being fluffed by Charlie Heggensford of Fluffers, Inc. At one set, he found himself sitting next to one of the other nominees, a man named Joe from the company Oral Agreement. Several of the actors decided to do a side by side "taste test" of the two fluffers, a move that made Charlie's stomach flutter with nerves. Afterwards, he was happy to hear that the actors had almost overwhelmingly preferred his technique compared to Joe's.

A few days later, Ken told Billy and Charlie about an industry party that he kept hearing rumors of on the sets of his movies.

"Industry party?" Billy asked in confusion. "Aren't they all industry parties?"

Ken shook his head. "This one sounds like a porn community party only. No outsiders allowed. That means it should be pretty hot."

"Hot how?" Charlie asked.

"As in anything goes." Ken waggled his eyebrows. "Who's up for it?"

"Are we invited?" Charlie asked, nervous about crashing a party that might get them in trouble with the people they worked with on a daily basis.

Ken sat back and looked at him with a frown. "Of course we're invited. We're part of the industry, aren't we?"

Billy nodded and shrugged at Charlie. "He's got a point. We've sucked as much cock as any of those actors."

Charlie nodded. "Okay. When is it?"

"Tomorrow night. I've got the address. It's a place in the hills that I've never been to before. I'll pick you both up at nine tomorrow night outside the office." Ken got up and stretched his arms over his head as he worked his jaw muscles. "Okay, I've got to get to work. See you later."

The following night, they were all crammed in the Beetle, winding their way through the streets above Hollywood until they located the address. A valet attendant gave them each the once over as they stepped out of the car and Charlie, feeling emboldened from his nomination, left him with a wink and a smile. The night seemed to be made for them.

The front door was standing open so they walked right in. A sunken living room was packed with people, mostly men, all in various stages of undress. Conversations rose and fell around them and smoke hung over the crowd like a bridal veil.

"Wow," Billy whispered, letting his eyes roam over the crowd below. "They're all so beautiful."

"Let's go mingle, shall we?" Ken suggested and they followed him down the steps.

Each grabbed a glass of champagne off the tray of a passing waiter and it wasn't until Charlie had almost turned away that he noticed the waiter wore only a silver lame jockstrap and matching shoes. Only in California could a person buy a silver lame jock strap and matching shoes.

Charlie made his way through the throng of people, casual hands reaching out to cup his crotch and ass and making him smile as he sipped his champagne. He could hear whispers as people pointed him out as the new fluffer in town who was nominated for The Hummer and tried not to swagger. By the time he came out on the other side of the crowd, his shirt was unbuttoned and flapped around him, exposing his chest and stomach. He was glad he did so many stomach crunches every night. Ken and Billy were nowhere to be found.

"Hey, it's my neighbor the fluffer," a voice said in his ear. Charlie turned to find Brent Harrington standing behind him. Brent had his shirt off and wore it tucked into the waistband of his jeans. His belly hung just slightly over the top of his pants, enough to give him a meaty look without making him look fat. The hair on his torso was soft, seeming to call to Charlie to run his fingers through it.

"Hi Brent," Charlie said as he grabbed another glass of champagne. "How are you?"

Brent nodded and grinned, his goatee stretching with the motion. "Just great. Made two more movies, paid my rent and I have some cash left over for fun." He drank from a can of beer he carried in his meaty fist and looked around. "Great party, huh?"

Charlie nodded and looked around as well. "I've never been to an industry party before. It's amazing."

They talked about life in the city and on the sets of their movies, exchanging tidbits about the people they knew at the party as they walked past. Charlie suddenly found he was out of champagne and also that he required more. Brent guided him through the crowd, his big hands on Charlie's shoulders and his bare belly pressing into the small of Charlie's back. They reached a long bar made up of glass block and both men leaned on it. A familiar looking young man, shorter with a stocky build, was serving drinks. He smiled at them and took their orders.

After receiving the drinks, Charlie and Brent turned to watch the crowd some more. Before he could sip from his drink, however, Charlie's hand was bumped by Brent's elbow and the drink splashed down his chest. He gasped at the icy feel of the wine spilling along his skin and down into his jeans as Brent grabbed a towel and began to dab at him.

"I'm sorry, Charlie," Brent said. He took the empty glass from Charlie's hand and set it on the bar. "I'm so clumsy."

Charlie laughed. "Trust me, you're not half as clumsy as I am."

A waiter with drinks walked by and Brent reached out to grab a fresh glass of champagne, handing it to Charlie with another apology. Charlie thanked him and leaned closer to say in Brent's ear, "I'm going to go look around. I'll catch up with you later."

Brent nodded and raised his can of beer in salute. He watched Charlie merge into the crowd and turned to glare at the bartender. Leaning over the bar, he said with a growl, "Try that again and it'll be the last drink you serve, you glorified cater waiter."

The bartender narrowed his eyes and snipped, "I don't know what the fuck you're talking about, you tub of hair. Get away from the bar and make space for two normal sized people, would you?"

Brent smiled at him. "You wannabes are so cute when you're angry. Hand it over."

The bartender sneered at him but, after assessing the look on Brent's face, rolled his eyes and surrendered a small bottle of clear liquid with which he had spiked Charlie's drink.

"Thank you," Brent said and pocketed the bottle. "Was it special for him or just random?"

The bartender flipped Brent off and turned his back. Brent scowled at the retreating man then pushed off from the bar and made his way through the crowd.

Charlie came upon a flight of stairs leading down to what sounded like a very full basement. He finished his drink and set the glass on a kitchen counter then descended into the noisy room. Men were kissing, groping, rubbing, and sucking each other in one large orgy of skin and sweat. They stood, straddled, squatted, and knelt around and on one another, their tongues and mouths sliding over skin glimmering with sweat. Charlie watched the action from the safety of a wall for a few minutes before noticing a separate room off in the corner. He edged around the orgy participants as his brain tried to catalog all the copulating he was witnessing. There was so much sex going on it was amazing.

A sling hung in the back room, suspended over mats that reminded Charlie of his days back in the elementary school gymnasium. A nude man lay strapped in the sling and another, larger man stood between his legs wearing leather chaps, a leather jockstrap, and a leather band around his biceps. The leatherman's arm moved rhythmically in the area of the sling rider's pelvis as his face hovered in the shadows cast by a single bare bulb hanging above the sling. Charlie stood on his toes and tried to see over the crowd of men watching the scene, but it was no use, they were all too tall. Had some college basketball team recently arrived at the party? He shifted position, working his way around the room, but found the view was no less informative. What was going on in the middle of this ring of people?

He backed up to try and see around one man's shoulder and bumped into a narrow table set against the wall. Testing the table, he decided it would hold, then climbed up on it to crouch with his head just below the ceiling. Charlie frowned and squinted, leaning forward and trying to see over the heads that kept shifting in front of him.

With a start, he realized he was watching the leather man slide his hand up into the anus of the man in the sling. He was actually watching a fisting scene live in the basement of this house. Charlie blinked. How could that big, hair flecked hand fit up inside that man's asshole? He felt his own sphincter tighten at the thought and he shuddered. It would have to be more painful than taking Samson's huge cock up his ass.

Thus distracted, Charlie did not notice how close to the edge of the table he was standing. It was that precarious position, along with the champagne he had downed upon his arrival, which caused him to fall forward into the crowd of men before him. As he plummeted through their ranks, he realized they were all masturbating as they watched the fisting. Charlie knocked several men down to the mat covered floor with him. The surprised men rolled apart and stood up again, grousing and swearing as they tucked their dicks away and stormed from the room. The remaining circle of men glared down at Charlie before turning back to the action still going on in front of them.

Charlie struggled to his feet, his head spinning from the fall and the wine. He stumbled a bit and placed his foot square on a glob of thick, creamy lube that had dripped from the wrist of the leather fister. Charlie's foot slid out from under him, moving into the circle of voyeurs masturbating around the participants. The toe of his shoe connected with the leatherman's anklebone, causing him to jump and let out a yelp. When he jumped, the fister inadvertently slid his hand further up inside his partner, effectively pushing him back on the straps that supported him. The man in the sling let out a cry higher in pitch to his partner's and raised his head.

With an audible *pop*, the fister, concerned about injuring his playmate, pulled his hand completely out of the asshole spread open before him. More globs of grease fell to the mat which further hindered Charlie's ability to stand upright as he fought to regain his balance. His foot went out from under him again and he fell to his knees before the tall, muscular man in the leather chaps. Looking up, he found Rock Harding standing before him, the pouch of his leather jockstrap at eye level as he peeled a greasy protective glove from his right hand.

"Charlie?" Rock said in surprise.

"Rock?" Charlie said. He noticed movement out of the corner of his eye and turned his head. The sling had hit the crest of its upward arc and now swung back downward, the angry red gash of the man's greasy asshole looming up in Charlie's face. He only had time to close his eyes before he felt the wet slap of the well-oiled hole collide with his face. The man in the sling jerked to a stop, his swing halted by the suction of his lubricated asshole striking Charlie's face. He let out a breathy, "Oh!" and raised his head to peer down between his legs. All he could see was Charlie's forehead and hair rising up over his groin.

The crowd gathered in the dimly lit room winced verbally and turned away from the gruesome sight. They tucked their cocks back in their pants and disbursed, knowing the entertainment, at least the fisting portion of the entertainment, had been waylaid.

"Oh God," Rock gasped. "Charlie!" He reached down and pulled Charlie's face away from the man's asshole. The two bodies parted with a soft sucking sound and the man in the sling began to sway once again.

"Oh God!" Charlie gasped, wiping at his face. "Oh, God!" He tried to stand but the slippery mat surfaces beneath him prevented the action. He fell forward into Rock's arms, his eyes squeezed shut as he blew strands of the greasy lube off his lips. "Oh, gross!"

Rock dragged Charlie out into the orgy room and kicked open the door to a small bathroom. He motioned the four people crowded inside snorting coke to get out, then dragged Charlie into the room and closed the door. Rock sat Charlie on the toilet lid and soaked a towel in the sink then began to wash off his face. As he wiped off the lube, Rock began to chuckle.

Charlie pried open an eye and glared at the man. "It's not funny."

Rock pursed his lips in an attempt to keep from laughing, but it was no use. The ridiculousness of the situation hit him again and he snorted, turning quickly back to the sink to rinse out the towel.

Charlie grinned in spite of himself. "It's really not funny. It's seriously . . . Well, it's disgusting is what it is." He chuckled and shook his head.

Rock risked a quiet laugh and glanced at Charlie out of the corner of his eye. Their eyes met and soon they were laughing loud and hard, wiping away tears and clutching their stomachs.

"You should have seen the look on your face just before that guy's ass hit you," Rock said through his tears. "Oh, I wish I had that on film."

Charlie laughed harder, imagining how it had looked from Rock's angle and remembering how it had looked and felt from his own. "I tell you, that guy needs to lighten up on the fiber, you know what I'm saying?"

They laughed for a few minutes more, then Rock surprised Charlie by reaching out to run a finger down the side of his face. "I'm glad to see you here. I was hoping you would have heard about the party and shown up."

Charlie smiled, feeling himself blush and hating it. "I'm glad to see you, too. I guess. I never knew you were into the whole fisting scene."

Rock shrugged. "I'm not. Cedric wanted me to do this to provide a little edge to the party."

Charlie frowned. "Cedric?"

Rock nodded. "Yeah. It's his party. You didn't know that?"

Charlie shook his head. "No, I didn't. Ken heard about the party while he was working a set, but none of us knew who was throwing it."

"Oh," Rock said. He scratched his chin, then shrugged. "Well, this is my house. Welcome to my home."

"You live here?" Charlie said. "It's so beautiful, no wonder you don't want to leave Cedric."

Rock waved his hand in a dismissing motion. "It's not all that. It's complicated." His face darkened for a moment, then his eyes lit up and he said, "Hey, do you want me to show you around upstairs?"

Charlie grinned and nodded. "That would be nice."

He followed Rock up three flights of stairs until they arrived on the surprisingly vacant third floor of the house. A large, handsomely decorated bedroom took up much of the floor. A smaller room across the hall held workout equipment, and another room further down contained a simple bed frame with mattress and several tall wardrobes.

"What do you keep in these?" Charlie asked as he ran his hand over the walnut finish of one of the wardrobes.

"Sex stuff," Rock replied casually. "Go ahead and look if you want." He turned to check his hair in the large mirror behind the bed.

Charlie opened one of the wardrobes and found several pairs of leather chaps, leather pants and leather vests hanging in neat rows. The smell of the leather mixed with Rock's sweat and unique citrus scent enveloped him in an intoxicating aroma. He wanted to press his face into the crotch of each pair of pants and breathe in the essence of the man behind him.

The other wardrobes contained more leather, some boots, and a small collection of leather masks with zippers. He lifted one mask out and looked it over. No eyebrows. Rock excused himself to go to the bathroom and Charlie replaced the mask. Not that he had thought Rock had been the prowler, but it was always better to be safe. As he was about to close the doors of the wardrobe the light caught the surface of another mask just right and he paused.

Charlie eased the doors open and reached slowly into the wardrobe. He grabbed the mask and lifted it off the shelf where it lay half buried beneath two others. As he turned it to the light, Charlie could plainly make out two arched eyebrows, white, painted over the zippered eye openings. His heart beat faster and his stomach turned just slightly. Rock owned the mask worn by the intruder at Fluffers, Inc.

"Oh, you like that one?" Rock asked as he returned to the room. "Cedric has a thing about Adam West, so I painted on those eyebrows one night as a joke." His face fell a little. "That was a while ago, though. I haven't had it out for a long time."

Charlie smiled, trying not to give away his feelings, and returned the mask to the shelf. He closed the doors to the wardrobe and turned to face Rock. He could barely bring himself to look at the man. What did this mean? Charlie knew he had to find Ken and get more information about the mysterious figure that had broken into the office. Could it have been Rock? Had he been using Charlie to get information for Cedric about Kinitia and Fluffers, Inc.?

"Charlie?" Rock asked. "You okay?"

Charlie blinked. "Huh? Oh, sorry. I guess I'm tired. I should probably head home. I've got a long day tomorrow."

"Oh." Rock's disappointment was obvious in his eyes. "Well, it was nice to see you again. It's been a couple weeks."

"Yeah, it has."

"That night at the mesa," Rock said quietly. "Remember?"

Charlie nodded and looked away. "I remember." He straightened up and clapped his hands together, a nervous trait he could remember seeing his father do a thousand times before. "Well, thanks for cleaning the lube and ass matter off my face."

Rock smiled a little sadly. "You're welcome. Thanks for livening up the party."

Charlie shrugged. "No problem. It seems to be what I do." He took a breath and headed for the door. "Good night."

"Hey, Charlie?" He stopped and turned. Rock smiled and said, "Congratulations on your nomination for The Hummer."

Charlie nodded. "Thank you. And congratulations on your nomination for Best Actor."

Rock nodded. "Thanks. I guess I'll see you at the awards ceremony then, huh?"

"Yeah. I'll see you there. Take care, Rock."

Charlie left the room and headed downstairs to find Ken and Billy. As he descended the steps, Charlie did not notice Brent Harrington walk quietly out of the exercise room and cross the hall to enter the room where Rock stood leaning against one of the wardrobes.

Rock looked up as Brent entered. "Everything go okay?"

Brent nodded. "You were right about the bartender. But it's okay, I caught it in time."

"What was it?"

"GHB." Brent handed over the bottle. "Don't know if it was random or if Charlie was targeted specifically."

Rock raised his eyes to the ceiling. "I had a feeling. Thanks for your help, Brent."

Brent shrugged. "Not a problem. It's a nice apartment and I could use the extra cash. Besides, I like Charlie."

"Yeah, he's special," Rock said softly. He looked up at Brent as if noticing him there for the first time. "Okay, you know what to do. Keep your eyes open."

"You can count on me." Brent left the room and walked down the steps, pulling his T-shirt on as he went. He would get another beer and then try to figure out where Charlie had gone.

11

VALET OF THE DOLLS

Charlie waded through the house, his eyes darting through the crowd of people. He needed to find Ken and Billy and tell them about the leather Batman mask in Rock's wardrobe. But they were nowhere to be seen. He walked all over the house, even back down to the basement. The orgy was still going strong, and to Charlie it seemed that more bodies had been added. He stopped to watch as an anonymous cock filled a gaping sphincter. The member slipped deeply into the orifice and Charlie took a breath, pulling himself away from the scene and into the back room where the sling had been hung. The back room was empty, void even of the man who had been lying in the sling. Someone had obviously found him and unbuckled his bindings.

Charlie ascended the steps, funneling his way through the crowd and out a large sliding door to the pool area. Several men were swimming around nude, their bodies glimmering in the white lights of the pool. Charlie stopped to gaze with child like glee at the free spirits gliding through the blue water, then turned away. He had to stay focused. This was important.

After walking around the back yard and interrupting seven different couples engaged in various sexual acts, Charlie made his way along the driveway down the side of the house. He stopped at the front corner of the house and stood with his hands on his hips. Where the hell were they?

"Looking for someone?" a voice asked.

Charlie turned and found the valet attendant leaning against a tree. His white shirt was unbuttoned to the middle of his chest, exposing a thin tuft of dark hair between his pecs. A trim goatee surrounded his mouth and his dark hair hung down over his forehead as he stood with a foot braced on the tree behind him. A cigarette glowed between his lips, lending him a B-movie bad boy image.

"Yeah," Charlie replied. "The two guys who came with me."

The valet blew out a soft cloud of smoke. "You were in the red Beetle, right?"

Charlie pulled his head back, surprised. "Wow, good memory."

The valet shrugged and flicked his cigarette butt off into the shrubs. "I've got a good memory for faces, especially pretty ones." The man strode past, lightly brushing Charlie's shoulder and staring him down with an unsettling and very arousing intensity. Charlie turned to watch the man scan the wooden pegboard holding the keys to every vehicle parked up and down the street. He tapped one peg in particular and turned back to Charlie.

"They're still here."

Charlie smiled. "Good. I was beginning to think I might have been ditched."

"A pretty boy like you?" The valet walked up and stood a few inches closer than standard etiquette allowed. "You're one of them, aren't you?"

Charlie frowned. "One of who?"

The valet jerked his head toward the house. "Them. The dolls."

"Dolls?"

"Yeah, dolls. They're all pretty and picture perfect, like dolls. They're all actors and actresses from porn movies, you do know that much don't you?" The valet gave him a sideways look.

"Well, yeah, I know that," Charlie replied a little defensively. "But I'm not a 'doll' as you put it. I've never been in a porn movie."

"Really?" The valet looked him up and down, then leaned forward to whisper quietly, "Small dick?"

Charlie's mouth dropped open and he stammered, "N-no! I have a nice sized dick, thank you."

The valet leaned back and regarded him from beneath hooded eyes. "What is it then? You're pretty enough."

Charlie blushed. "Well, thank you. But I haven't been asked to be in a movie. If you must know, I'm a fluffer."

The valet's eyes widened. "A fluffer? Really?"

Charlie straightened his back a bit and replied, "Yes, really. Is there something wrong with that?"

The valet stood smiling at him, a hand over his mouth as he stared. "Huh? Oh, no. No, there's nothing wrong with that. I'm just very . . . Well, I'm very intrigued."

Charlie cocked an eyebrow. "Oh?"

"I've always wondered how good fluffers were at sucking cock." The valet looked around, then reached out and took Charlie by the hand. Walking quickly, the valet crossed the large parking area off the driveway and approached a brand new BMW. He opened the door and folded the driver's seat forward to crawl into the backseat.

Charlie hesitated outside the door. What if someone came outside to get their car?

"Come on," the valet hissed from the darkness of the backseat.

"What if someone wants their car?" Charlie whispered back.

"It's still early," the valet replied. "No one's leaving yet."

Charlie hesitated a little longer, then slid into the car. The valet reached over him and pulled the door shut with a quiet, solid thump. The soft leather upholstery caressed Charlie's arms and wrapped lovingly around his ass. He had never sat in such a luxurious vehicle. The overhead light dimmed then went out and they were left in the darkness of the car's interior.

"I'm Jared," the valet said as he scooted closer.

"Charlie." He felt the first tentative brush of Jared's lips and smiled. "Your lips are soft."

"Thanks." Jared gently turned Charlie's head and pressed his lips against Charlie's mouth. He slid his tongue out and pushed insistently against Charlie's teeth until they parted and granted him access.

Charlie could taste the light tobacco from the cigarette Jared had been smoking and the tang of it sent a shiver down his spine. Their kiss deepened, mouths biting each other sensuously as their tongues rolled together. Charlie's shirt, still unbuttoned, slipped easily off his shoulders and soon both men were nude and sprawled across the warm leather of the seat.

Jared ran his tongue down Charlie's neck to suckle softly at his throat. He raised Charlie's left arm and ran his tongue through the hair of his armpit, continuing on to hover over his left nipple. He began to pull at the tender bud with his teeth, bringing it up to a hard knob of sensitivity in seconds.

Charlie groaned and pressed a hand against the back of Jared's head. He could feel the hard line of Jared's erection lying along his thigh and moved his leg back and forth to rub against the blood-gorged organ. Jared shifted between nipples, moaning against Charlie's chest.

After working over Charlie's nipples, Jared moved down to his navel and slipped his tongue into the shallow orifice. Charlie gasped and lifted his hips, giving Jared the opportunity to slip a hand between his thighs and start rubbing the crack of his ass. Tracing his tongue down through the hair of Charlie's belly, Jared swallowed the length of Charlie's cock in a single gulp, pressing his nose and lips into the aromatic bush of Charlie's groin.

"Oh, God," Charlie whispered. "Suck that cock down."

Jared lifted his head and looked up at Charlie with a smile. "You're right, you don't have a small dick."

Charlie smiled back at him. "Thanks."

Jared swiveled his hips to straddle Charlie's face, offering up his own cock as he began to feast on Charlie's meat. Reaching up, Charlie grabbed the long cock in his hand and stroked it slowly as he evaluated the organ. Jared was almost exactly Charlie's size and shape. His balls, dangling just over the bridge of Charlie's nose, were larger and Charlie opened his mouth to suck them in. He stroked Jared's cock and sucked his balls with his nose pressed up against the hairy perineum of the valet's ass.

Jared grunted in appreciation around his mouthful of dick. Charlie continued to suck his balls, breathing in the heady aroma of the man's ass and testicles while he stroked the length of his cock. He released Jared's balls and, with a final lap of his tongue, slid down to take the length of the man down his throat.

They sucked each other for several minutes, both men feverishly working his hot mouth up and down the dick before him. Jared pressed his index finger up against Charlie's asshole and moved it in a small circle. Charlie returned the favor, sliding his finger through the hair of Jared's ass crack and massaging the twitching pucker of muscle he longed to fill with his cock.

"Oh, that feels so good," Jared groaned. "I want to fuck you, Charlie."

"Oh yeah, I want to fuck you, too," Charlie said.

"I can do two loads close together," Jared offered. "Can you?"

"Oh, baby," Charlie replied with a grin. "You have no idea."

They shifted positions and Jared retrieved a condom from a pocket of his pants then rolled it up over his cock. Charlie was on his knees, his head on his arms on the seat with his butt in the air. Jared ran his tongue along the crack of the ass before him, then slurped at the precious hole that quivered beneath his tongue. He slipped a finger up inside, then drooled gobs of spit down into it, working the saliva deeper with each push of his finger. Satisfied with his preparations, Jared moved up and aimed his cock at the opening barely visible in the lights from the house. He pushed into Charlie and felt the muscles of the fluffer's ass part before the crown of his dick then constrict around the shaft.

He stopped halfway in and eased back out. Charlie groaned into the seat and bit down on his forearm when Jared moved forward again. The man's slender, rock hard dick plowed slowly between Charlie's tight ass cheeks, spreading the flexible sphincter as his cock was buried completely in Charlie's body.

"Oh, God!" Charlie groaned. "Fuck me, Jared. Pound my ass."

"You got it, baby," Jared replied and began to pump his hips. His rhythm increased until his cock was a veritable piston of energy pounding into Charlie's hole. "Oh, you've got a hot ass, fluffer man."

"Fuck that ass," Charlie gasped. "Fuck it. Oh, shit. I'm cumming!" Charlie lifted up off the seat and jerked himself to climax, the cum spraying out over the leather interior of the new BMW.

"Oh, fuck," Jared said in Charlie's ear. "I'm going to shoot inside you."

"Cum on, baby," Charlie replied. "Cum up inside that ass."

Jared emptied his load into the condom and rested his head on Charlie's shoulder. Sweat ran down their bodies as they caught their breath. When his breathing had returned to normal, Jared whispered, "Ready for round two?"

Using his underwear, Charlie wiped up the cum as best he could, then moved to kneel between Jared's legs as the valet stretched out on his back along the seat. Charlie placed his hands under Jared's ass and lifted his hips. He tightened his grip on Jared's ass cheeks, spreading them apart and effectively popping open the wrinkled pink sphincter. Lowering his face, Charlie dabbed his tongue into the moist, sweat ripened hole and began to spit into it. He licked and sucked Jared's asshole, lathering it with saliva and slipping a finger up inside.

Before long Charlie was hard once again and paused to stretch a condom along the length of his cock. He pressed up against the threshold to Jared's body and slid into the man, driving deep into the hot, wet tunnel. Muscle wrapped around his cock and stroked it lovingly. Charlie groaned and turned his head to run his tongue along the sweaty, hairy skin of Jared's calf.

"Oh, fuck!" Jared cried out, his fingers digging into the leather beneath him. "Jesus, Charlie, you're going to split me in half!"

"Not quite," Charlie said with a grin. "But I'm going to try."

Jared laughed and raised his head. "Okay, fluffer. Go for it."

Charlie winked and braced himself, raising his hips and beginning to move them, slowly at first then picking up speed. He ended up crouching on the seat of the car with Jared practically standing on his head, jackhammering into the stretched asshole beneath him. The car bounced and shook from the force of Charlie's pile driving fuck.

Jared took the brunt of Charlie's forceful fuck with a stunned expression. His eyes were squeezed shut and his mouth hung open as his ass was pummeled into submission by Charlie's prick. Charlie shifted position and Jared felt the underbelly of the cock banging into his ass brush up against his prostate, pushing him over the edge. He opened his mouth wider and caught the majority of his own load as it spurted from his dick.

"Oh, fuck," Charlie grunted. "That was so fuckin' hot. I'm going to cum, oh yeah." Charlie pulled out of Jared's raw, red ass and peeled off the condom as the first load of semen shot out of his cock. He covered Jared's balls and perineum with his cum, pressing his sweaty back up against the roof of the car as he stroked himself through his orgasm.

They regained their composure and kissed for a little while. Charlie wiped up as much spunk as he could find using both pairs of underwear. Jared slowly pulled on his pants, his ass a little sore and his leg muscles cramped from the fuck he had just endured.

"You're a machine," Jared said with a sigh. "That was amazing."

Charlie shrugged. "I was inspired."

Jared smiled at him. "Really?"

"Sure. I've never fucked in a BMW before." Charlie laughed at the thunderstruck expression on Jared's face. "I'm just kidding."

They finished getting dressed and climbed out of the car. Leaning back inside, Charlie sniffed warily and looked at Jared with a guilty expression. "It smells pretty rank in there."

Jared shrugged. "So? If they can afford a BMW they can afford to have it detailed. Come on. You've got to find your friends and I need to piss."

Charlie parted company with Jared at the line to the bathroom. He made his way through the crowd of people in the living room and stopped at the glass block bar. The same young, stocky bartender was taking orders. He smiled at Charlie and approached him.

"What'll it be?" the bartender asked with a sexy smile.

"Champagne," Charlie said. He turned and scanned the crowd, hoping to see Billy or Ken coming toward him.

"Here you go. Enjoy." The bartender winked and walked off down the length of the bar to take care of other people.

Charlie picked up his glass and was about to take a sip when someone bumped his shoulder. The wine upended and ran down his bare chest, a repeat performance of the last glass of champagne he had ordered from the bartender.

"Jesus!" Charlie yelped. He looked up and found Brent Harrington looking at him with a guilty expression. "For God's sake, Brent, put a bell on your neck or something!"

Brent laughed and took the empty glass from Charlie's hand. He stripped off his T-shirt, once more exposing the soft, hairy belly that Charlie found oddly arousing, and began to wipe the champagne off Charlie's torso.

"Better?" Brent said into Charlie's ear.

Charlie battled off a tingle as the man's goatee brushed up against his ear. "Thanks."

"Sorry I spilled your drink."

"*Again*," Charlie added with a laugh.

Brent nodded and accepted the addition. "Again. Here, let's get you one from that waiter over there." Brent took Charlie by the arm and practically pulled him away from the bar and into the crowd. He grabbed two glasses from a scantily clad waiter and handed one to Charlie. Raising his in a toast, Brent said, "To new friends."

"And neighbors," Charlie said. They touched glasses and drank. Brent made a face and shook his head, causing Charlie to laugh and almost spit the wine out his nose. "Don't like the champagne?"

Brent shook his head. "Not really. I like beer and good wine." A passing waiter allowed Brent to place his glass on the tray of empties.

Charlie turned his head slightly and caught sight of the back of Billy's head as he walked up the steps across the room. "Oh! Dammit! There's Billy. I've got to talk to him. See you later, Brent."

"Bye Charlie." Brent watched Charlie make his way through the crowd and up the stairs. When he was sure Charlie was gone he shot the bartender a withering look and headed up the stairs as well.

Charlie caught Billy at the end of the hall. Billy turned, looked at him blankly for a moment, then smiled and threw his arms around Charlie's neck, squeezing him tight. "I love you!" Billy cried out.

"Okay, Billy." Charlie struggled to unlock the man's arms from around his neck. "I'm glad to see you too." He looked closely at Billy's face and asked, "What did you take?"

Billy shrugged. "A small pill."

"Ecstasy," a man passing by said to Charlie. "And a lot of champagne. I saw him do it."

"Yeah, you wish!" Billy called after the man, then hugged Charlie again. "I love men."

"Yes, Billy, we all do." Charlie stood him up and looked around, trying to decide what to do. A familiar face appeared in the crowded hall and he called, "Brent! Can you help me out?"

Brent took one of Billy's arms and Charlie took the other and together they guided him to the stairs.

"Do you know anything about Ecstasy?" Charlie asked Brent. "Like how long the buzz lasts?"

"I took Ecstasy!" Billy called out in a sing song voice.

Brent shook his head. "Never touch the shit. I have enough trouble with reality without fucking up my brain with drugs."

"Good reasoning," Charlie replied. They got Billy outside where he fell on his back onto the thick lawn. He pulled up tufts of sod and tossed them into the air, laughing as the clods rained down on his face and chest.

"Good Lord," Jared said, walking up to stand between Brent and Charlie. Billy was laughing hysterically and rolling on the grass.

"Yeah." Charlie looked up at the house then turned to Brent. "You weren't about to leave, were you?"

Brent shrugged. "I'm pretty much over the whole scene. Want a ride?"

"Do you mind taking him home first?" Charlie nodded to Billy.

"No problem." Brent looked over at Jared. "I've got a . . ."

"Green Subaru Outback," Jared said. "I remember. Be right back."

Brent raised his eyebrows and looked at Charlie. "Good memory."

"Yeah, he is," Charlie said with a grin. A clump of sod hit him in the chest, the dirt mixing with his sweat and the last vestiges of champagne and he turned to glare at Billy. "I'm going to tell you every detail of this night tomorrow morning." Billy stuck out his tongue and continued to roll in the grass.

The car rolled up and Jared helped them get Billy in the backseat. As he held the door for Charlie, Jared winked at him and asked, "Is he one of them?"

Charlie glanced in at Brent as the bear fastened his seat belt. "Yeah, he's one of them."

Jared nodded. "I can see it in him. Have fun. I'll tell your friend you made it home safe."

"Thanks, Jared." Charlie got in the car and Jared closed the door. He stood and watched the vehicle roll slowly down the drive.

In a third story window of the house, Rock Harding stood silhouetted against the light from the room behind him. His hands were clasped behind his back, the small bottle of GHB held in the palm of one hand. He would use it to question Cedric when the time was right, but not tonight.

He watched Brent's car move slowly down the driveway and, with a flash of brake lights, disappear up the street.

12

Ultimatum

Three days after the industry party, Charlie found himself on a set for a beach movie. The main scope of the movie was taking place in a modern, airy beach house with additional scenes filmed on and around the beach itself. He contemplated the past few days as he waited between jobs. He had not yet told Ken and Billy of finding the Batman mask in Rock's closet. For some reason, he hadn't been able to bring himself to tell them, still feeling conflicted himself over what it might mean. He did not think Rock was directly involved with the break in, but the mask proved that he was on the fringes of whoever had been in the office.

To distract himself, Charlie entered the house through a sliding glass door and looked around. The house was bright and open, a spacious set in which to film a movie. Charlie walked through the rooms with a gleam in his eye. The furniture had been carefully chosen to be comfortable as well as decorative. The kitchen was a wide expanse of stainless steel appliances and gleaming white countertops. And this was someone's idea of a simple summer home.

While gazing at the artwork on the walls, Charlie inadvertently tripped over a thick shag run the color of the carpet and fell with a *thump*. He lay on the rug for a moment, embarrassed, then raised his head to look around. Had anyone seen him?

The entire cast and crew of the movie were staring at him. His fall had interrupted the filming of a scene and as he watched the two actors started to lose their hard-ons.

"Cut!" the director snapped. He was a newcomer to the field, someone young and eager to make himself known. With his hands on his hips he marched over to Charlie and leaned down to peer into his face. "Are you on drugs?"

"What?" Charlie asked. He stood up quickly, too quickly, and wobbled as he experienced a head rush. "Woah."

The director gasped. "You are on drugs, aren't you?"

Charlie narrowed his eyes and glared at the man. "No, I'm not on drugs. I'm clumsy. Ask any of these guys, they'll tell you."

The director turned to the actors on the sofa behind him and they nodded. "He is pretty clumsy," one of them said.

"But he sucks cock like there's no tomorrow," the other offered.

Charlie shot the actor a dark look, then looked at the director as the man turned back to him. "See? Just clumsy."

"Hmm. We'll see." The director walked back over to the camera, noticed the limp dicks on his actors, and sighed, waving them off toward Charlie for fluffing. He stepped outside on the wrap around deck to have a cigarette and talk on his cell phone, completely ignoring the ocean spread out before him.

Charlie gently sucked and stroked the men back into tumescence, his eyes half closed with pleasure. Above his administrations, the two men talked about the upcoming awards ceremony.

"I bet Cedric gets the fucking thing again this year," said the shorter of the two.

"Really?" the other replied. "I would have thought Rod might have a chance this year."

The shorter one snorted. "Have you seen the drivel he's been putting out? A lot of story, plot development, and attempts at character development. And a lot of shots of feet. What's with that?"

Charlie smiled around the man's dick, recalling the dinner he had spent at Rod's house with the director under the table eating his meal off Charlie's feet. The sex afterwards had been really good, too.

"Feet, huh?" The taller actor chuckled. "Hey, did you hear about what happened at Cedric's party?"

"No, I wasn't able to go. What happened?"

"Someone had sex in the backseat of Cedric's new BMW and left spooge and sweat all over the upholstery. He had to have the thing professionally cleaned. He was pissed. And right before the awards." The men laughed as Charlie choked and began to cough. It had been Cedric's car! The taller actor reached down and tousled Charlie's hair. "Well, we all know who's going to take home The Hummer, right Charlie?"

"Well ..." Charlie said.

"Yeah, he's sucked all the right cocks," the shorter, and now seemingly snottier, actor said.

"Okay ladies," the director called. "Are you ready for your close ups?"

"Yes, Mr. DeMille," the men replied in unison and walked off, leaving Charlie kneeling on the rug in mid suck. He wiped the spit from around his mouth and carefully sat in a chair to watch the scene. He grinned as he thought about the sex he and Jared the valet had had in Cedric's car and what they had left behind. Funny how things worked out.

Across the room the actors were performing oral sex on each other, stretched out along the couch in a 69 position. The taller actor managed to suck his partner's cock all the way to the root with each stroke, while the other man began feasting on the taller actor's asshole. He licked, sucked, and speared his tongue into the smoothly shaved hole, poking deep into the man with the tip of his tongue. The taller actor groaned around his mouthful of cock and reached around to slip a finger up inside the asshole just beneath his nose.

After a few more minutes of filming, the director called, "Cut!" and the men eased out of their position. Turning, the director looked back at Charlie and said, "Fluff them until we change camera angles."

Charlie moved into the scene and began to suck the men, his mouth and tongue sliding easily over the large, thick cocks.

"Come on, fluffer," the shorter, snottier actor said. "You can take it deeper than that." He began to thrust his hips, pushing his cock further into Charlie's throat.

A competitive need to show this man what he was capable of overcame Charlie's sensibilities. Forgetting everything Ken had taught him, Charlie started to suck the man's cock harder. He reached out and took the taller actor in his hand, stroking him in time with his oral rhythm.

"Oh, yeah," the taller actor groaned. "Keep that up, fluffer."

Charlie forgot himself, his surroundings, and the actors. There existed only these two dicks and his hands and mouth. He sucked greedily at their cocks, moving his mouth up to fasten on the cap of velvety skin on the head and then lowering it over the entire length of the shaft. The men moaned and bucked their hips beneath him, pulsing into his mouth and fist.

Before he knew it, Charlie felt the man beneath him stiffen up. The shorter actor gasped and managed to utter, "I'm cumming."

Charlie backed off from the now erupting cock and let the warm semen splash over his face. His fist was still pumping along the hard muscle of the taller actor's dick and he turned to begin sucking on it. It did not take long for him to bring this man to orgasm as well, moving away just in time for the actor's seed to spurt up into his face.

"Oh, fuck," Charlie said. He could feel hands on his cock and wondered when his pants had been pulled down his thighs. He leaned back and rode the actors' fists to a gusher of an orgasm, panting and gasping as he fought to catch his breath afterwards.

"Wow!" someone said from across the room and Charlie blinked his eyes open. The director and cameraman were standing there, both with stunned looks on their faces. "Charlie, that was really fucking hot."

"Huh?" Charlie looked over the two actors reclining before him. "Oh, fuck. I'm sorry. Oh, shit."

"No, no, no," the director said and approached him with a large towel. "Here, clean yourself up."

Charlie wiped up as best he could, then reassembled his clothes and met up with the director in the kitchen. The actors were sharing a shower off in another part of the house.

"Look, I'm really sorry I did that," Charlie said. "I haven't made someone cum in a long time."

The director smiled. "Charlie, I want to make you a deal."

"A deal?"

"Yes. I want to pay you so I can use that scene in my movie."

Charlie frowned. "What scene?"

"The one I just finished filming with you and John and Corey." The director smiled.

"You . . ." Charlie stopped, his blood running cold. "You filmed that?"

"Yes!" The director clapped his hands. "It was great! Do you have any idea how hot you were?"

Charlie shook his head, stunned. "No."

"You were very hot. So fucking hot I can almost see the movies flying off the store shelves. Every gay man in America will want to whack off while watching your scene."

"I . . . *My* scene?" Charlie paused. What was happening? "I didn't want to be filmed. I was just doing my job."

"Well, from where I was standing, it looked like you were over performing." The director's smiled slipped a bit, becoming cooler, more dangerous. "Would you like me to report this to the other directors? I could you know. Then what would happen? Do you think you would be able to get work anymore? This isn't the kind of thing a director wants to happen on his set without his approval."

Anger flickered through Charlie's eyes. "That's blackmail."

"No, honey," the director replied. "It's life. Think it over. You have twenty four hours." He presented Charlie with a business card and headed back into the living room. "Is that cleaned up yet? Where are those bitches? Someone go get them out of the shower before they cause a water shortage."

Charlie hung his head and left the beach house, not even bothering to get his time card signed. What had he done now? Just when he thought everything was going so well, he had to go and do something stupid.

He caught a bus back into town, staring out the window and ignoring the other passengers. If he allowed the scene to be used, he might get other acting jobs, which would be okay, he guessed. He didn't really want to be a porn actor, though, he was happy being a fluffer. Aside from that, the thing that was really bothering him was he hadn't known he was being filmed. It wasn't the fact that the scene had been caught on tape, it was the manner in which the director had gone about it. He had been dishonest. And then he had given Charlie an ultimatum. What was he going to do? Whatever his decision was, he would have to make it in twenty-four hours.

Charlie thought about it the rest of the morning and was happy to see his neighbor Brent Harrington walking around in a pair of boxer shorts when he showed up at another job site that afternoon.

"Hey, Charlie," Brent called. He walked over, the length of his cock swaying beneath the cotton boxers. "It's good to see you."

Charlie smiled. "Hi Brent. Good to see you too."

"How's Billy doing?"

Charlie nodded. "He's okay. The Ecstasy wore off by the next morning and he was back to being himself." Charlie looked away, distracted by his inner contemplation.

"Hey, something wrong?" Brent asked, his black eyebrows knitting together in concern.

"Well, sort of." Charlie told him about being filmed and the ultimatum the director had presented to him. "I've thought about it and really don't want to be an actor. Not right now. I just want to be a fluffer, you know? But the main issue I have with this whole thing is the way he went about it. It almost feels like a setup."

Brent nodded, scratching his goatee. "It does sound suspicious. What's this guy's name?"

Charlie fished the card out of his pocket. "Ian McCloud? I've never seen or heard of him before."

Brent took the card and flicked a corner thoughtfully. "Let me ask around, check this guy out for you. I'll let you know tonight what I find out."

Charlie's mood lifted a little. He had help; he wasn't alone. "Really?"

"Yeah. I like you." Brent turned to watch the scene being set up. "Oh, I've got to be in that scene in like ten minutes. Think you can get me up?"

Charlie grinned. "My pleasure." He knelt before Brent and reached into the fly of his boxers. He slid the man's cock out through the split in the fabric, then pulled his balls out as well, letting them hang outside the fly. Opening up, Charlie took Brent's dick deep in his throat and began massaging it with his tongue, his hands gently kneading the man's balls.

"Oh, man," Brent sighed. "That feels nice." He stood with his legs apart and his head tipped back as Charlie brought him to full erection. The director called out Brent's name and the hairy man reached down to gently touch Charlie's face, looking down at him with a soft expression. "Thanks, Charlie."

"You're welcome," Charlie replied. He watched Brent walk across the room, shucking his boxer shorts as he went. Reaching up, he touched his cheek where Brent's hand had lingered and pondered the feelings the man's touch had brought up. Rock usually touched him like that after Charlie had finished fluffing him, maybe it was just some left over feelings for Rock. Or maybe the sweet bear of a man who lived across the hall from him had managed to get beneath his skin?

Looking after Brent, he watched the man prepare himself for the upcoming scene. Brent rolled a condom over his dick, lubed it up and waited for the director to call, "Action!" before stepping up to the man kneeling before him on all fours. After a few teasing jabs, Brent sank his bulky dick between the other bear's hairy ass cheeks and began pounding away. His thick fingers gripped the loose skin around his acting partner's hips and he tipped his head back as he pulled out and plunged back in. His thick cock furrowed the man's asshole as the bear grunted and gasped beneath him.

Charlie turned as another big, hairy man walked up and presented himself for fluffing. He licked his lips, trying to keep his erection from distracting him, and leaned in to begin his work.

Later that night, Charlie's phone rang as he was getting out of the shower. He wrapped a towel around his waist and answered it just before his machine picked up. It was Kinitia Jones.

"Just wanted to let you know we have an extra ticket for the award ceremony tomorrow night," Kinitia said.

"An extra one?" Charlie asked. "Why?"

"Tony has to go to Las Vegas for an emergency fluff session. I thought since you were the only Fluffers, Inc. team member who was nominated you might want to bring a date."

Charlie snickered. He'd been so busy fluffing half the men in the community he had barely had time to date. Unless he counted the dinner at Rod Mandrake's house. Or the one dinner he had had with Rock. Or maybe that night he had spent with Rock on top of the mesa.

"Charlie?" Kinitia said suspiciously. "You're not thinking of asking who I'm afraid you're thinking of asking, are you?"

"What? Who?" Charlie asked, a bit too quickly for him to be innocent of Kinitia's accusation.

"Rock Harding, that's who," she shot back. "You stay away from him unless you're working on one of his sets, got that? He is trouble in the most serious way. Not just for you, but for the company as well."

"I know that," Charlie snorted. "I wasn't thinking about Rock." *Very much*, he thought to himself. "I was just trying to think if there was anyone I wanted to invite."

At that time a knock sounded on his door and Brent Harrington called out, "Charlie, it's Brent."

"You know, Kinitia," Charlie said as he turned to the door. "Hold on to that ticket for me. I'll let you know if what I have in mind actually works out."

"It's not Rock?" Kinitia asked.

"No, it won't be Rock Harding." Charlie said good bye and opened the door, still in his towel.

Brent's eyes traveled the length of Charlie's body, a glimmer of interest sparking in their dark depths. He took in Charlie's hairy calves built up from work on the Stairmaster, the bulge beneath the slightly slipping towel, the flat, hairy surface of his belly and the broad expanse of his hair covered chest. His eyes finally met with Charlie's and Brent could not contain his grin. "Am I interrupting?"

Charlie smiled, suddenly feeling self-conscious. "No. I just got out of the shower. Come on in."

Brent walked past him, glancing down along Charlie's body one more time, and leaned against the small kitchen counter. "Well, I found out some more information about your sneaky director."

"Like what?" Charlie started pulling clothes from his dresser drawers, turning his head to indicate he was listening to Brent.

"He's linked pretty closely with your all time favorite director, Cedric Wilmington." Brent grinned at Charlie's shocked expression. "Seems Ian McCloud worked as a crewmember on a lot of Cedric's movies and has wanted to become a director for a long time. But Cedric always shut him down, telling him he wasn't ready for the responsibility, that kind of stuff. Until just recently."

"It was a setup! But why?" Charlie pulled his underwear on under the towel and then discarded it. It was odd, he had sucked Brent's cock and seen the man nude on the sets of his movies, but getting dressed before him just seemed too intimate. "Why would Cedric even want me to become a part of a movie? You would think he would want to keep me down in the ranks with the fluffers and not let me succeed." He shook his head. "It's weird."

Brent nodded. "I agree." He tried not to watch too closely as Charlie walked around the room in his underwear. "Well, that's what I came to tell you. Guess I'll let you get on with your evening."

"Oh, hey," Charlie called to him. He was pulling on his jeans and, distracted by Brent's attempted exit, fell on the floor.

"Jesus, Charlie," Brent crossed the room and helped him up. "You okay?"

Charlie nodded with a blush. "Yeah, just clumsy as usual." He sat on the edge of his futon and pulled on his jeans. "I wanted to ask you a question. Are you going to the Golden Orifice Awards tomorrow night?"

Brent shook his head. "Nah. I'm not nominated and none of the guys I work with are, so I was just going to watch some TV. Why?"

"Well, I've got an extra ticket and would really appreciate it if you would go with me."

"Really?"

"Yeah."

"Like a date?"

"Well . . ." Charlie looked away, his head spinning. Was that what he wanted? "Yeah. As a date. I just . . . we live so close together, across the hall, you know? And it's a little awkward. But it would be nice to be with someone I think of as a close friend." Charlie raised his eyes. "Does that make sense?"

Brent looked at his face for a long moment, then smiled. "It does. And I accept. What time?"

Charlie gave him the specifics and hugged him. "Thanks, Brent."

"No, thank you." Brent turned to go to the door where he paused with his hand on the knob. "I need a tuxedo, don't I?"

Charlie's eyes widened. "Oh, God, so do I!"

Brent laughed. "Well, let's go. Get dressed and knock on my door when you're ready."

"Okay," Charlie said and started running around his apartment looking for his clothes. The phone rang just as he was heading out the door and he hesitated. Should he? He swore quietly and picked it up. "Hello?"

"Charlie, it's Ian McCloud."

Charlie narrowed his eyes. The sneaky director. "Oh, hi Ian."

"Hmm," Ian said. "I take it from your tone that you've decided not to sign the waiver to allow me to use your scene."

"That would be correct."

"Well then," Ian replied. "You should be at the board of directors meeting for the Golden Orifice Awards tomorrow morning at nine a.m. There's a motion before the board to have your name stricken from the ballots for the Hummer award."

"What?" Charlie gasped. "Why?"

"Apparently you've appeared in a film, therefore you are considered an actor and not a fluffer. I have been asked to contribute my footage to build a case against you before the board of directors."

"Wait a minute. Board of directors of what?" Charlie asked.

Ian sighed. "A number of directors in gay porn sit on a board. We collect the nominees for the Golden Orifice Awards as well as the Hummer. We also have veto power. One of the members of the board has made a motion to have your name removed from the ballots. Be there tomorrow at nine sharp if you want to present your case, otherwise don't even bother to show up at the awards."

Charlie flinched at the click in his ear when Ian disconnected on him. He hung up the phone, his blood pressure rising, and stormed out his door to pound on Brent's.

"Hold your water," Brent said as he crossed his apartment. Charlie stomped past him when he had opened the door, stopped in the middle of the room, and turned with his hands fisted on his hips.

"Do you know what that fucking asshole of a director just said to me?" Charlie told Brent of the pretty much one sided conversation he had just completed with Ian McCloud and was satisfied to see the bear before him get worked up as well.

Brent, however, could hold his temper better than Charlie. "We'll take care of this, Charlie. Trust me. We'll be there tomorrow at nine a.m., and then we're going to that awards ceremony and your name is still going to be on that ballot. Let's go get our tuxes and then I'll make some phone calls."

"Who will you call?" Charlie asked.

"Friends. Come on." Brent ushered him out the door and closed it behind him. As they descended the steps, Brent thought to himself that the whole situation stunk of Cedric Wilmington.

13

Bored of Directors

Charlie and Brent arrived at the offices of Four on the Floor pictures a few minutes before nine the day of the awards. The studio, one of many specializing in gay porn, was hosting the meeting in deference to one of the studio's top directors who was also Chairman of the Board for the Golden Orifice Awards. They sat in chairs against a wall and looked around the sparsely decorated conference room, taking in the posters of porn films produced and released through Four on the Floor and the cheap Formica conference table surrounded by office surplus chairs. Charlie hoped this would not be a long meeting as the chair he was sitting in was severely uncomfortable. He shifted his weight and tried to find a more agreeable spot on the cushion, but it was useless. He may as well have been sitting on a bag of rocks.

The door opened and a line of men entered the room. They were grumbling about the early hour and cast sleepy glances at Charlie as they filed past. They took their seats around the conference table and Charlie caught a wink and a smile from Rod Mandrake. Several of the other directors he had worked for gave him a smile as well, which allowed him to relax just a bit. Maybe Cedric was full of hot air after all. The chairman brought the meeting to order and turned to nod to Cedric.

Cedric stood up from his chair and leaned on the table, looking each of the directors in the eye. "We have a problem with one of our fluffers."

"Cedric," Rod snapped. "We're all tired, we all stay up way too late at night to have the patience for a long morning meeting. Please skip the *Inherit the Wind* theatrics and get to the point."

Cedric leveled a cool look at Rod, but lifted his chin and strode to the front of the room. A VCR and TV stood in the corner on a stand with wheels. He stuffed a tape into the VCR and switched on the TV. Static played for a moment, followed by a blue screen, then a shot of a dim restroom. A man walked into the frame and entered one of two stalls. The camera was placed up in the ceiling, effectively able to film the occurrences in both stalls at the same time. Charlie frowned as he watched. What movie was this and why was it being shown?

And then he recognized himself about the same time the directors all recognized him as well. It was the restroom he had stopped at to jerk off after he had fluffed Rock by the waterfall. Charlie lowered his head into his hands and shook his head. The sound was bad, barely heard sighs and grunts, and the lighting was dim, but Charlie and the man with the uncut cock could be seen well enough to know what they were doing. He watched his performance with a sick feeling in his stomach. The directors watched the scene with interest until the cum shots at the end. The screen went dark after Charlie left his stall and walked off camera.

Cedric punched the TV power button off and turned to address the room. "So, you see, the fluffer is not a fluffer at all. This is from a movie entitled *Barrio Bathroom Jocks*. It was released two weeks before the nominations were announced."

The directors all shifted position, realigning their hardened dicks after viewing the scene, and glanced at one another. The chairman, an older man Charlie had worked with once, looked down the table at him and asked, "Charlie?"

Charlie stood up, his knees almost buckling with nervousness. "Yes sir?"

"Were you a willing participant in this scene?"

Charlie hesitated. "Well, I was not forced to have oral sex with that man, if that's what you're asking, but --"

"Thank you." The man looked at the directors around him. "I would like some input before we vote."

Ian McCloud stood up, avoiding Charlie's eyes. "I would like to state that Charlie caused several disruptions on my set and, I know, many other sets. He was also adamant that he had wanted two of my actors to reach orgasm when I asked him about a fluffing performance I inadvertently filmed on the set of *Beach Blanket Butthole.*"

"That's a lie!" Charlie exclaimed, rising to his feet. "He tried to blackmail me with that scene."

Ian let out a snort of laughter. "I do not blackmail people."

"Charlie, sit down," the chairman instructed. "You'll get to have your say."

Charlie took his seat, wincing as one of the cushion's lumps pressed against his tailbone. Brent reached over and reassuringly patted his knee.

"Any other comments?"

Rod Mandrake spread his hands before him. "Charlie caused problems on a few of my sets as well, but I have to give him credit. I would never have gotten the kind of sun rise scenes and reworked the scene like I did in *Anally Yours* without his interference. I felt he was professional and respectful at all times."

Charlie smiled, recalling each of the times he had worked for Rod Mandrake. Rock Harding had been part of the cast of each of Rod's movies and Charlie felt a warm tingle at the thought of the man, even though it had been Rock's influence that had caused him to stop at that restroom.

"I move to have his name stricken from the ballot," Cedric said and slapped his hand on the table, causing them all to jump.

"Oh, for God's sake, Cedric," the chairman snapped. "Act like a real person for once, would you? And no one uses the word 'stricken' any longer." He shook his head, then looked down the table at Charlie. "Charlie, what would you like to say to these charges?"

Charlie stood up and cleared his throat. "I'd like to say that I was filmed without my knowledge and that I have never been contacted to give my permission to allow anyone to use that footage. As for my performance on the set of *Beach Blanket Butthole*, I would like to say that I became overworked while performing my fluffer duties and *accidentally* overexcited the men I was servicing. I apologize for it." He sat back down and gave Brent a tight smile.

"All right then, if there are no more comments, we can vote . . ."

The door swung open and Rock Harding strode into the room. Charlie's eyes widened at the sight of him and he turned to Brent who shrugged under his questioning look. Rock pulled a young, stocky man into the room with him, his long, strong fingers wrapped around the man's biceps.

"I have a comment," Rock stated.

"What?" Cedric cried out and turned to the chairman. "Call for order or something!"

"Uh, Rock," the chairman stammered. "This is a closed meeting."

"Not for long." Rock turned and stopped Cedric from rising out of his seat with a cold glare. "Sit down, Cedric. Brad here has some things to tell all of you." Rock pulled Brad in front of him and stood looming over the man. "Brad?"

The young man cleared his throat and cast a nervous glance over at Charlie. A spark of recognition flickered in Charlie's mind as he realized Brad had been the bartender at Cedric's industry party a few days ago.

"I, uh . . ." Brad swallowed hard and fought to find his voice. "I have to admit to something."

"And what might that be, Brad?" Rod Mandrake asked, sitting up straight to check out the man's feet.

"What does this have to do with the decision looming before this board?" Cedric cried.

"Cedric," Rod snapped. "Shut up." He turned and assessed the nervous young man who looked so small before Rock. "Please go on."

Brad cleared his throat and took a breath. "I was the other man in the scene in the restroom. I knew about the camera in the ceiling and I intentionally entered that bathroom to entice Charlie into having sex." A low murmur arose from the directors. The chairman raised his hands for silence and nodded for Brad to continue. "I was also directed to try to drug Charlie at the industry party at Cedric Wilmington's house."

"Drug me?" Charlie turned to Brent. "Was that . . .? You kept spilling my drinks."

Brent returned his look, his dark eyes serious, and nodded. Charlie turned back as Brad continued to speak.

"And I broke into the offices of Fluffers, Inc. to get specific information concerning the financial status of the company. I wore a leather mask and went through the papers in the front desk until I found the information." Brad hung his head.

Silence hung heavy over the group, then Rod asked the all important question on everyone's mind. The answer to the question that could result in a member of their board being turned out of the community and black balled from the industry. A pretty tragic situation considering it was, after all, a community of adult video creators and actors. "Brad, you say that someone asked you to do these things. Who was that person?"

Brad took a breath and raised his chin to look Rod Mandrake in the eye. Charlie held his breath and leaned forward with wide eyes as did the others in the room. Who would want to cause him such pain?

"I have no idea." There was an audible release of breath and the directors all slouched in their chairs. No life altering decisions would be required of them today. The relief was palpable as they adjusted their positions and murmured among themselves.

The chairman at the end of the table shook his head, his eyes a little more sad than relieved. "In light of these revelations, I move that all motions before this board of directors be dismissed. Anyone second?"

Rod raised his hand, his cold eyes fixed on Cedric. "I second."

"All those in favor?" Hands rose around the table, even Ian McCloud who avoided looking at Cedric or Charlie. "Opposed?" Cedric's hand was all alone. "Motion dismissed. Meeting adjourned. I'll see everyone at the ceremony tonight. Good luck to all who are nominated, including you Charlie."

Charlie smiled at the man. "Thank you, sir." He leaned over and hugged Brent tight, then stood up and approached Rock. Brad had slunk out the door the minute the meeting had ended.

"Hi there," Rock said.

"I don't know what to say," Charlie managed. "I can't thank you enough. How did you figure all this out?"

Rock shrugged. "Well, I kept hearing rumors about something going on, but I could never pin down the person who initiated it all. Plus, I couldn't let this happen to a good person whose company I truly enjoy." He noticed Cedric crossing the room toward them and said quietly, "I need to talk with Cedric. I'll see you tonight?"

Charlie nodded and watched Rock walk up to intercept Cedric's march. Charlie knew Cedric was behind all of it, but there was no proof he could provide to the board. At least not without also involving Rock by telling them of the mask in his wardrobe. And he did not want to do that. He turned to find Brent behind him.

"Ready to go and prepare for your big night?" Brent asked.

"You have no idea." They left the room and headed back to their building.

That evening, Charlie was trying to figure out which way his cummerbund should be worn when Brent knocked on his door. He opened it and gasped. Brent was dashing in a black tux with blood red tie and cummerbund. His hair was styled and his goatee neatly trimmed. He gave Charlie a rakish grin and sauntered in the room.

"You look great," Charlie said. "Wow."

"Thank you." Brent turned in a circle. "And may I say that you look like quite the appetizer as well?"

Charlie blushed. "Thanks. I feel completely frazzled what with the meeting today and all. I still can't believe Rock managed to get that guy to confess to everything."

Brent smiled. "Rock can be very persuasive."

Charlie narrowed his eyes and assessed his date. "You talk like you know Rock pretty well."

Brent shrugged. "I've worked with him on a few movies."

"Really?" Charlie briefly contemplated what a scene between Rock and Brent might look like and decided he would need to locate those movies for more thorough research. "Okay, I'm ready."

"You're gorgeous." Brent stepped up and leaned forward to lightly kiss Charlie on the mouth. "As your date for the evening, I am officially treating you like the star you are as of this moment on."

With a smile plastered on his face, Charlie followed Brent out the door and down the steps. Outside the door of the building, a limo stood waiting at the curb. A hot young stud of a driver stood holding the door open, a lascivious grin on his face.

"Good evening, gentlemen. I'm Doug and I'll be at your service tonight." His voice was deep and smooth as honey.

"Thank you, Doug," Charlie said and slipped into the large backseat. "This is amazing! You rented this for the night?"

"Not me, but a close friend of yours who wishes to remain anonymous." Brent pulled Charlie to him and kissed him, lightly at first and then more insistently. "If you're nervous, I can help you relax a little before we get there."

Charlie nodded. "I'd like that."

Brent kissed him again, his tongue making slow circles through Charlie's mouth. Brent's lips were soft beneath the fur on his face and his whiskers tickled. Soon the tuxes were removed and they reclined across the bench seat in the nude. Brent's heavy, hairy body felt sturdy and warm as it lay across Charlie's and he ran his hands along the man's broad back and down over his furry ass.

Brent shifted the focus of his mouth down to Charlie's neck, then moved to his nipples, nipping at each one until it was red and throbbing. Charlie groaned and pressed Brent's face down into his chest as he ground his leaking cock against Brent's thigh.

Sliding further down, Brent used his tongue to lift Charlie's oozing cock from his belly and slurped it into his mouth. He slowly let the blood gorged organ slide into his mouth, his tongue massaging it as it moved deeper into his throat.

"Oh, Brent," Charlie sighed. "That feels so good."

With his nose and mouth pressed into the bush around Charlie's groin, Brent moved a hand down between Charlie's legs and began to stroke the pink circle of his sphincter. Charlie shifted his hips to allow Brent a better angle and reached his own hand down to grab the solid pole jutting out from Brent's groin. Before he had worked Brent up to erection and then watched him walk away; now he would get to start with Brent's hard-on, work on it until he came, then watch it soften afterward. A nice change.

Brent moved his hips and climbed up on the seat to allow his pelvis to hover over Charlie's face. Charlie opened his mouth and raised his head to take Brent's stout cock into his throat. Running his tongue along the shaft, Charlie gently massaged the pulsing dick. He tasted a smear of pre cum, the flavor working to turn him on even more.

They sucked each other for several minutes, the only sound that of their contented sighs and the slurping of their actions. Charlie savored the clean taste of Brent's freshly showered cock, the smell of his soap rising from the pubic hair into which he repeatedly immersed his nose. Brent's hairy belly hung down and scraped up along Charlie's chest with each thrust of his hips, the hair brushing up against his sensitive nipples and making Charlie squirm.

Charlie released the cock in his mouth and slid lower, coaxing Brent to plant his hairy ass right down on his face. Spreading the big, solid cheeks open he feasted on the tender ring of muscle buried beneath Brent's body hair. He could taste the sweat of sex and smell the clean aroma of his skin. He lapped at the puckering hole, sliding his tongue up into the hot confines of Brent's ass.

"Oh, yeah," Brent grunted. "Eat that big hairy ass. Yeah, get your tongue up in me."

Brent raised Charlie's legs and moved his mouth down over Charlie's asshole. He sucked at the rosy pink button, slurping and spitting into it. With his thumbs planted on either side, Brent popped Charlie's anus open then drove his tongue straight into the man. Charlie groaned up into Brent's ass as the bear's tongue pierced him. He doubled the suction and speed of his tongue, flicking it quickly in and out of Brent's hole.

"That's it," Brent said and slid off of Charlie and pulled him upright. "I gotta have that big dick up my ass. You need to fuck me, and I mean now."

Charlie leaned back against the seat and kissed him, twisting Brent's nipples while Brent reached around for his tuxedo pants. He pulled a string of condoms from the pocket and Charlie laughed.

"Were you expecting me to be an easy lay?" Charlie asked.

"I was hoping." Brent opened a condom, then leaned down and sucked Charlie's dick, leaving it slick with spit. He rolled the condom over Charlie's cock, then straddled his waist and slowly impaled himself. Charlie looked up and noticed a tiny mirror over the bar across from him. He watched as his thick, hard cock disappeared up inside Brent's body with each bounce. Reaching around, he spread the cheeks of Brent's ass open and could see the point of insertion more clearly. Brent's sphincter was stretched around the shaft of Charlie's cock and he felt his body respond to the image. He had never watched himself fuck someone before.

"Sit on that big dick," Charlie said and groaned as the bear on his lap ground his pelvis down to take his cock even deeper. Charlie leaned forward and caught one of Brent's nipples between his teeth and pulled on it.

"Oh, yeah," Brent grunted. "Bite that tit. Suck my tit. Oh, fuck yeah."

Brent's rhythm picked up and before long he had jerked himself to climax. His load spurted over Charlie's chest and belly, slathering him with a thick layer of cum. Charlie reached down and grabbed the thick cock around its base as he pounded up into Brent's ass. A few moments later he closed his eyes and shot his own load up into the tip of the condom buried deep in Brent's body.

"That was great," Brent whispered and leaned down to kiss Charlie gently on the mouth. They disconnected and Brent flopped over onto the seat beside Charlie, both men catching their breath.

"That was really hot, guys," the driver called back. "There's some towels by the bar for you to clean up."

Charlie felt himself blush. He had forgotten all about the driver. Brent chuckled at the pink in Charlie's cheeks and moved up to grab some towels. They wiped up and then got dressed, helping each other with their bow ties and cummerbunds.

Charlie finished tying his shoes just as the limo pulled up to the large banquet hall hosting the awards ceremony. The driver jumped out and opened the door. Charlie and Brent stepped out into the waning afternoon light and walked along the concrete path to the lobby of the banquet hall. A few other limos were scattered around the parking lot, but for the most part people had simply driven themselves. SUVs and higher priced vehicles took up most of the spaces in the lot.

The lobby was spacious and tastefully decorated. As they walked across the deep pile carpet, Charlie saw Kinitia, Ken, Billy, and the rest of the fluffers waiting to enter the main room.

"Hey! It's the star of the night," Kinitia said and hugged Charlie.

"Hi everyone," Charlie said with an embarrassed grin. "This is Brent Harrington."

Greetings were made all around and they filed into the hall. Ken leaned over to Charlie and asked, "Did you like the surprise I sent you?"

Charlie frowned at him, then understood. "The limo? That was you?"

Ken smiled proudly. "Hand picked the driver myself."

"That was really nice of you, Ken. But you didn't have to do that."

"I wanted to. You're a good kid and you deserve to have some fun." They took their seats at a table off to the side and Charlie looked around. The fluffer companies each had a table and all the movie studios seemed to have two or three for themselves. The hall was large, decorated with fresh flowers and linen table cloths. A large stage with a dais took up the front of the room and several large screen monitors had been placed at strategic points.

As he took it all in, Charlie saw Cedric Wilmington and Rock Harding enter the room. Rock was beautiful in a white tuxedo with black bow tie and cummerbund. He trailed a few feet behind Cedric, talking to the other cast members of the movie for which he had been nominated. Charlie felt his heart jump a little at the sight of him. The man had such a vibrant physical presence.

"He looks good, doesn't he?" Brent whispered, nodding to Rock.

Charlie smiled and looked away. "Yeah, he does. But he's not who I'm with tonight."

Brent grinned at him. "I for one am very glad of that."

The lights dimmed over the attendees and the stage lights came up. The chairman of the board of directors who had headed up the meeting that morning walked across the stage and Charlie felt the first of many butterflies. The evening was just beginning.

14

And The Hummer Goes To...

The awards were handed out with great fanfare. Charlie sat at the table surrounded by his friends, the odd little clutch of people who had come to feel to him like family. They laughed at the jokes people made, the slurred acceptance speeches, and the pratfalls of the emcee, a young gay comedian who was quite taken with having the honor of handing out the awards.

The final awards, the most prestigious, were left for last. The Hummer was a follow up award that would be given out at the very last, following Best Picture.

"Well, here we find ourselves in the home stretch," the comedian announced. "I for one know I'm going to need to stop in the bathroom on the way out . . . so I'll see half of you in the last stall." A round of laughter followed, louder from the tables that had consumed more alcohol. Charlie thought briefly of the scene he had unwittingly contributed to *Barrio Bathroom Jocks*, then pushed the memory out of his head. Tonight was for fun, no negativity allowed.

The emcee began reading the nominees for Best Actor in a Gay Video. Charlie crossed his fingers beneath the table and risked a glance in Rock's direction. A flutter of excitement jumped in his chest as he caught Rock staring at him. He smiled and held up his crossed fingers and Rock nodded and returned his smile. Charlie noticed Cedric sitting a few seats away from Rock, talking to the person next to him and completely ignoring the emcee and everyone else at the table.

As each name was announced the monitors played a segment of non-sexual acting followed by another segment showing the man in full sexual action. Rock was nominated for his role in the movie *Back Nine*. Charlie had not yet seen the movie, but as he watched Rock's acting ability he found he was surprised at the man's talent. Rock seemed to be able to really play a role without having to resort to sex talk and his impressive physical presence. Then the scene changed to show him battering a young, upturned ass and Charlie's dick sprang to life. Rock's face was tipped up and one of his large, hairy hands rested on one of his partner's firm, pale ass cheeks. Grunts and groans crackled through the monitors as Rock's large cock plunged repeatedly into his on screen partner. Charlie shifted position and glanced to see if Brent had noticed his arousal. To his relief, Brent was engrossed in the scene himself.

A loud round of applause followed Rock's scene and he nodded graciously. Charlie noticed that Cedric was still talking to the man next to him, completely oblivious to the ceremony around him and his supposed lover's moment in the spotlight.

"And the Golden Orifice goes to . . ." The emcee opened the envelope and smiled. "Rock Harding for *Back Nine*!"

Wolf calls, whistles and applause followed Rock up to the stage where he took the award, a tall, bronze phallic shaped object, and hugged the emcee. He leaned down to speak into the microphone, thanking the other members of the cast, especially the man he had been working with in the scene just shown, as well as the crew. Rod Mandrake had directed Rock in the movie and he gave a special thanks to Rod, telling him he was eager to work with him again. Before he left the stage, Rock turned and locked eyes with Charlie, his stare intense and his smile bright. Charlie smiled and raised his hand to wave which caused him to knock over his wineglass and send red wine all over the white tablecloth. His friends at the table erupted into laughter and he blushed. Looking back at the dais, he was disappointed to find Rock had already left the stage. Their moment had been brief, but a moment nonetheless.

"Nice move," Billy snickered.

Charlie shrugged and blushed deeper. A waiter appeared and whisked the offending wineglass away, blotting up most of the wine with a napkin. He reappeared with another glass of wine to place before Charlie, which Ken moved further into the center of the table out of Charlie's immediate reach. Charlie gave him a narrow eyed look, but smiled.

"And now it's time for Best Director of a Gay Adult Movie." The emcee read the nominations and when he got to Cedric's name Charlie looked over to find the director was suddenly the picture of attentiveness. Typical.

"And the Golden Orifice goes to . . ." The emcee let the silence spin out. Charlie hoped Cedric would go home empty handed and worked to keep his face neutral. "Rod Mandrake for *Back Nine!*"

Rod ran to the stage and leaped up to the dais. He was laughing and hugged the emcee tight. Charlie caught Rod looking over the emcee's shoes and knew he was trying to decide whether the man's feet were attractive. Rod made a happy acceptance speech including the entire cast and crew and the other directors for inspiring him to continue to grow creatively.

Brent leaned over as Rod stepped down and the applause started. "It's a regular industry love in tonight, isn't it?"

Charlie laughed and nodded, keeping his eyes on Cedric Wilmington. The director looked angry at having been shut out of his award and kept glancing at the statue standing on the table in front of Rock's place setting. Charlie felt a little thrill of justice and excused himself to go to the restroom. The presentation of the award he was nominated for was coming up soon and his bladder was bulging from nerves.

He found the men's room remarkably empty and sighed as he released a steady stream of piss. After zipping up, he turned around and stopped. Rock Harding leaned on the counter at the sinks, his arms folded and a crooked grin on his face.

"Hi!" Charlie said in surprise. "How long have you been there?"

Rock shrugged. "Few minutes. You nervous?"

Charlie nodded. "A little. Hey, congratulations! You're the best actor."

"Thanks."

Their silence hung in the air, pregnant with sexual tension. Charlie nodded then approached the sink and stood beside Rock as he washed his hands, trying not to breathe in the man's scent. It was impossible, however, to avoid the tangy, citrus smell of him. It wasn't overwhelming, just persistent and unique. He took a breath to clear his mind as he held his hands under the dryer, then turned to face Rock.

"So, going to any parties after?" Charlie wondered.

"Rod's having a party for the cast and crew of *Back Nine*. Would you like to come? I'm sure he'd let you in."

Charlie shrugged. "Ken rented a limo for me so I'm kind of hanging out with the guys from the office tonight."

Rock looked deep into Charlie's eyes. "And Brent Harrington."

"And Brent Harrington." Charlie nodded.

"He's a nice guy."

"Very nice."

Silence again. "Well, I guess we should get back out there," Rock said and gestured to the door.

"Yeah, I guess we should." Charlie stepped forward at the same time Rock stood up from the sink and he collided with the tall, muscular actor. A small puddle of water on the floor took his left foot out from under him and he fell against Rock, his arms going around the man's waist as his face pressed into the actor's hard, flat stomach.

"Woah there," Rock said with a chuckle. "You okay?"

Charlie nodded into Rock's stomach, ashamed to show his face. How could he be so continually clumsy around this man? "I slipped."

"I see that." Rock helped him stand up, then leaned down and kissed him very softly on the mouth. "For luck."

Charlie looked up into Rock's eyes for a long moment, the attraction between them evident. Then the door swung open, clipping Charlie's shoulder and sending him falling into Rock once again. Billy stepped into the room and looked at the two with raised eyebrows.

"Charlie, your award is being announced." Billy looked up at Rock. "Congrats on the win."

Rock smiled patiently. "Thanks." He steadied Charlie, then held the door open for them and followed both men back into the hall.

The emcee was just starting to read the names when Charlie and Billy reclaimed their seats. Each table burst into cheers when a member of their fluffing team was announced, but Charlie felt his table was the loudest. The studio tables all laughed and clapped with the members of Fluffers, Inc.

"And The Hummer goes to . . ." The emcee looked at the card and everything slowed to a standstill. Charlie could feel the seconds tick past, each longer than the one before it. The few seconds the emcee hesitated felt like five years. Brent had grabbed his hand under the table during the reading of the nominees and had just squeezed his fingers when the name formed slowly, oh so slowly, on the emcee's lips.

"Charlie Heggensford of Fluffers, Inc.!"

The people around him erupted into screams and applause. Everyone hugged him as he sat in stunned silence. He had won? He had actually won? He stood up and promptly fell to the floor, disappearing from view as he landed flat on his ass. Laughter and applause followed and someone shouted, "That's Charlie for you!"

More laughter followed and Charlie himself was laughing, blushing and crying as Brent helped him up and got him headed in the right direction. He climbed the steps with exaggerated caution and the crowd laughed again. The emcee carefully handed him the award, a mini version of the Golden Orifice, then quickly stepped away.

Charlie approached the dais, leaned forward, and bumped his front tooth on the microphone. More laughter as feedback whined through the speakers. He could see Kinitia, Ken, Billy, Brent, and the rest of his work family practically shaking with laughter and lying across the table, still stained with the wine he had spilled. He waited for the laughter to die down, then said, "I feel like Sissy Spacek in *Carrie* for some reason."

A round of applause and understanding nods. After it had died down, he looked at his table of friends and said, "When I arrived in LA from Idaho, I tried to find a job in which I could make a difference and find some satisfaction. Kinitia Jones was kind enough to give me the chance to make her proud and I hope I have done so."

"Baby, I *love* you!" Kinitia shouted and everyone laughed and applauded.

Charlie grinned and blushed. "Thanks." A gentle wave of laughter followed his simple response. "I want to thank my very good friend Ken Carlton for teaching me the art of fluffing. Billy Ransom for reminding me to stay young and foolish for as long as I can. Brent Harrington for acting as my guardian angel . . ." He turned and looked for Rock, finding the man standing at the back of the hall with a large smile on his face. "And those very special people who have made this city feel more like home than I ever could have imagined. Thanks again to all of you."

Charlie carefully descended the steps and returned to the table. Brent grabbed him in a bear hug followed by Ken, Billy and last of all Kinitia who had tears in her eyes.

"Farm Boy, you make me laugh, lose my temper, and love life all at once. Come here and hug me, dammit." Charlie hugged her tight and kissed her sleek, ebony cheek. "Thanks for believing in me."

"Uh uh, honey," Kinitia said. "You first believe in yourself, and then others will follow. Tinitia told me that a long time ago."

The tables were put away and the dance floor exposed. A DJ began to play music and the lights were dimmed. Couples moved out onto the floor and danced drunkenly, groping and touching. Charlie and Brent danced for several songs, as did Ken, Billy and Kinitia.

As the hour grew late, Kinitia's energy began to fade. Charlie noticed her sitting slumped in a chair at one of the few remaining tables and pointed her out to Ken.

"We should get her home," Charlie suggested. Ken nodded in return and they all collected their belongings, took Kinitia's arms and headed for the exit.

As he left the large, loud hall, Charlie turned back to take one last look and sighed, the Hummer cradled in his arm. It had been just as he had imagined. What a perfect evening.

Looking around the room he searched for Rock's familiar form but could not locate him. He had probably left early to attend Rod Mandrake's party. After one more visual sweep of the room Charlie followed his friends to the limo waiting down the block.

They dropped Kinitia off at her apartment and watched her weave her way up the walk to the door. Ken then directed the driver, Doug, to his apartment and they all went inside, Doug included.

Ken had a two bedroom apartment, the majority of space in both bedrooms taken up by a king sized bed. Ken handed each man a beer and they stood at the living room window looking at the lights of the city spread out below. Brent stood directly behind Charlie, his erection pressing into the crack of Charlie's ass and his hands in the front pockets of Charlie's pants.

"So, Charlie," Ken said and turned with a grin. "You going to share your hot, hunky date with the rest of us?"

Charlie grinned at the three men watching intently, then turned his head to look at Brent. "What do you say, big bear?"

Brent turned his head, resting it on Charlie's shoulder, and looked the three men over. "They're okay. I could go for them."

Charlie looked at Ken. "You heard the man. Lead the way."

They all filed into one of the bedrooms and began pulling clothes off each other. Mouths met and tongues entwined as masculine, hairy hands kneaded muscles and fondled hardening flesh.

The men stretched out on the bed, their bodies a vision of diversity. Doug had a solid, smooth body. His nipples were small and sat high on his hard, square pecs. Charlie immediately began sucking at the brown points of flesh as he sprawled across the bed on his stomach. Ken spread Charlie's ass cheeks wide and leaned down to begin rimming his hole with deep strokes of his hot, wet tongue.

Billy and Brent toppled onto the bed, their mouths sucking sensuously and their arms wrapped around each other as their hands tweaked and grabbed flesh. They rolled across the mattress as one until they bumped up against Doug. Brent, lying on top of Billy, turned his head and began kissing Doug, his goatee scratching over the clean-shaven skin around the driver's mouth. Billy slid down the length of Brent's body and coaxed him up to his hands and knees then took his hard, sturdy cock in his mouth.

Charlie moved down and held Doug's cock in his palm, running his tongue along its length and assessing its dimensions. Doug was well hung, about eight inches, and wide. Charlie breathed in the smell of the man's crotch sweat, then took half his cock in one swallow. Doug groaned into Brent's mouth as Charlie began sucking him with abandon.

Ken covered his long dick with a condom from the nightstand, lubed himself up and plunged deep into Charlie's hungry hole. The sphincter spread wide to take the entire length of Ken's cock and when he was buried completely inside Charlie's body, leaned forward to plant a kiss on the small mountain range of Charlie's spine. He pulled back, then began to pump steadily into Charlie's ass. His thighs banged against the firm cheeks of Charlie's ass, the gentle waves of muscle urging him to occasionally slap one or the other.

Billy rotated his body on the bed and turned his hips, presenting his cock and balls to Doug. The driver moved away from kissing Brent to take Billy's dick in his mouth and began to suck. Doug's moans leaked out from around Billy's seven-inch organ as Charlie continued to suck his cock while submitting to Ken's ass fucking.

Brent lowered his head and, as he fucked Billy's face, began to suck at Billy's balls while Doug sucked Billy's cock. Brent licked his index finger and slid it down along Billy's perineum and into his twitching hole. Billy moaned around Brent's cock and lifted his hips so that Brent could begin to finger fuck him with a steady rhythm.

Ken eased himself out of Charlie's ass and pulled the condom off his cock then tapped Brent on the back. Brent got up and rounded the bed to stand behind Charlie. He massaged the man's ass, spreading his cheeks wide and fingering the gaping hole. He pulled a condom from the drawer, applied it, then lubed up and slipped into Charlie's dark, hot cavity. With his dick embedded in the man, Brent leaned over his back and reached down to begin jacking Charlie off. Charlie grunted around his mouthful of Doug's cock, and began gyrating his hips around Brent's prick.

Brent raised up and began to grind his hips in the opposite direction, twisting his cock in the confines of Charlie's tight hole. Charlie released Doug's cock and looked back over his shoulder at the hairy man standing behind him. "Oh, God, Brent. That feels really fucking good. Keep fucking me."

"You like this big bear cock up inside you?" Brent said and tossed his sweaty hair out of his face.

"I love that big cock up my ass. Get it deeper in there. Fuck me. Oh, yeah!" Charlie bent back to Doug's cock as Brent began to bang into his ass, fucking him steadily.

After several minutes, just before he might get close to orgasm, Brent pulled slowly out of Charlie and stripped the condom from his dick. Billy jumped up then and got behind Charlie. Before long he was thrusting into Charlie as well, his dick bumping steadily against Charlie's prostate. Charlie could take no more. He raised his head and grunted as he blew his load onto Doug's crotch. His cum covered the driver's cock and balls. When he was finished, Charlie leaned down to lick and suck his own cum from Doug's body.

After Charlie had cleaned the cum from Doug's dick, the driver stood up and took his turn at Charlie's ass. He filled Charlie's gaping hole even more, stretching the ring of muscle wide as he fucked the lube slick hole. Charlie rode Doug's cock with his head in Brent's lap and the bear's dick down his throat. Billy and Ken stood on the bed to either side of Brent and the man divided his oral attention between them.

Doug's rhythm slowed down and he finally pulled free from Charlie's asshole, leaving the orifice red, raw and glistening with lube. The men shifted positions and Ken lay on his back on the bed, his covered cock sliding up into Doug's tight pink hole. Doug rode Ken's dick for some time, bouncing over the man's groin and taking the long, thick cock to the root each time. Ken slowed to a stop, his dick buried up in Doug's ass, and nodded to Brent. The man stepped up behind Doug, rolling a condom down over his cock and smearing lube on its length. Doug leaned down over Ken's torso and moaned as Brent pushed himself up into Doug's hole alongside Ken's dick.

Ken squeezed his eyes shut and let out a groan as the bear's cock crammed into the tight orifice beside his own. Brent let out a breath and put his hands on Doug's shoulders, then both men began to pump into him. Doug rode their cocks as sweat poured down his body. His leg muscles stood out with the exertion of crouching on the mattress.

Charlie stepped up behind Brent and slid a lubricated finger into the man's asshole. He slowly searched the warm tunnel until he found Brent's prostate and began to massage the area. Brent turned his head and kissed Charlie deeply, their tongues rolling over each other. When he came, Brent moaned the words, "I'm going to shoot," into Charlie's mouth. He grunted through his orgasm, then pulled slowly out of Doug's talented ass.

Billy moved up to take Brent's place and slid into Doug on top of Ken's big cock. The two men began to pump a steady rhythm into the limo driver who finally reached his own limit and shot a long, thick string of cum up over Ken's head to spatter across the sheet.

Ken came inside Doug's ass and remained lodged up inside the man as Billy pulsed to his orgasm. The men eased themselves free from the driver then all five collapsed onto the bed.

A few hours later, Brent, Charlie, and Doug walked unsteadily down to the limo. Billy had opted to remain at Ken's for the night. Brent and Charlie climbed into the back seat and dozed off as Doug drove them home. They gave him a large tip, plus their phone numbers, and headed up the steps. Charlie invited Brent over once the man had changed his clothes and took a quick shower himself while he waited. He placed the Hummer on his small entertainment center and turned off all the lights except for a string of glowing chili peppers draped along the wall. The surface of the award caught the red and green of the peppers and reflected the light around the room.

Brent knocked a few minutes later and they tumbled into Charlie's futon. They stripped out of their boxers and lay nude in each other's arms, talking quietly.

No work was scheduled for anyone involved in the porn industry the following day, having been declared an annual industry holiday several years before. Everyone was going to be too tired, hung over, or both to be able to function. Charlie and Brent decided to head to the beach and cruise the married men on vacation with their families.

With a smile, Charlie drifted to sleep against Brent's hairy chest.

15

Tying Up Loose Ends

Two days after the Golden Orifice Awards ceremony, Charlie entered the office of Fluffers, Inc. to find a large, energetic woman answering the phone. She had curly dark hair, shoulder length, and a round face with round, plastic framed glasses. She was speaking rapidly in a northern Minnesota accent and scribbling notes on Post Its. Every available surface of the area around her was covered with Post Its. Charlie smiled and she flashed him a bright, endearing smile then immediately began talking with the person on the other end of the line.

He wandered down the hall and found Kinitia in a spare room he had never been inside. Charlie had assumed the door led to a coat closet or storage room. Instead, it opened into a spacious, empty room that smelled of new carpet. A tiny bathroom was situated off to one side. Kinitia was sitting in a folding chair at a card table, her head bent over a mass of paperwork and her extensions hanging down over her shoulders.

"Wow, nice room," Charlie said.

"Oh, Farm Boy!" Kinitia jumped up and threw her arms around his neck. "How are you? Did you enjoy your holiday?"

He told her about his day spent at the beach with Brent and she smiled. "He seems like a nice guy."

Charlie shrugged, embarrassed, and replied, "He is. But we're just dating. Nothing serious."

Kinitia giggled and headed back to her card table. Charlie approached and glanced over her shoulder. She was making up schedules for her team of fluffers. There seemed to be quite a lot of demand all of a sudden.

"Excuse me, Ms. Jones?" the woman from the front desk poked her head in the door. "There's a phone call you may want to take. From a studio head."

Kinitia smiled. "Okay, Bernice. I'll be right there. Oh, Bernice, this is Charlie Heggensford."

"Oh, hi!" Bernice extended her hand and shook Charlie's warmly. "I'm Bernice Tallipepper. It's nice to meet you." A distant phone rang and she dashed off.

"Where did you get her?" Charlie asked with a grin.

"A temporary service."

"Does she know what we do here?"

Kinitia shrugged and smiled. "I don't know. But she's been doing a great job all morning. I checked the machine yesterday and had thirty eight messages, so I decided to arrange for a temporary receptionist to help out." Kinitia stood up. "And I'm taking over this empty room. Until we move."

"Move?" Charlie gasped. "Oh no, Cedric is forcing us out?"

Kinitia waved her hand at him with a relaxed look. "No, no, no. That burglar you told me about may have seen the lease, but he wasn't a very thorough burglar. My lease is up in six months. I'm going to look for a new office. We need to expand anyway." She giggled again and left the room to take the call.

Charlie shook his head and headed back to the waiting room. Ken and Billy were snuggled up on the couch watching *Dirty Dancing*. They looked over and smiled when they saw him.

"Hey there, hot stuff," Ken called. "Come join us."

Charlie sat on the floor with his back up against the sofa and pulled Ken's arm around his shoulders. Billy reached out and rubbed his neck.

"Did you guys have a good day off yesterday?" Charlie asked.

"Oh yeah," Billy snickered. "We didn't leave Ken's apartment all day."

Charlie turned around with a smile. "Really? And does this mean anything?"

Ken shrugged. "Just that we're having a really fun time." Billy nodded his agreement. "How about you, Farm Boy? How's your hunky bear friend?"

Charlie grinned and nodded. "Good. We went to the beach and then out to dinner."

"And then?" Billy asked.

"Stuff." Charlie turned back to the movie and smiled as he thought about Brent. He was a nice guy.

"Um, Charlie?" Bernice said in a timid voice. He stood up and found her hovering in the door with a piece of paper. "I'm sorry to interrupt, but Kinitia said this is a really hot job and the director asked for you specifically."

Charlie took the note from her. "Okay. Thanks Bernice."

The phone started to ring again and Bernice trotted up the hall, her hips swinging beneath polyester pants. Charlie shook his head, then waved to Billy and Ken and left the office. He decided to splurge on his first day back as an award winning fluffer and flagged down a cab.

The address was for a bar across town called The Bronco. Charlie paid the driver, then stepped into the cool, dark bar. The room was wide with pool tables and pinball machines scattered around. A long bar sat against the back wall, the mirror behind it dimly lit by track lighting.

"Charlie!"

He turned to see Ian McCloud waving to him. Charlie's eyes narrowed in annoyance. First Ian had tried to ruin his career and now he had requested Charlie to work on his set?

"Ian," Charlie said in a cool voice. He walked up to the man and stood before him with his arms folded. "Doing another movie so soon? Need some additional footage or something? Is that why you requested me?"

Ian shrugged and laughed nervously, then took a breath and said, "I'm really sorry about the beach house thing. I never should have done that. Please accept my apology. I wanted to put things right between us."

Charlie assessed him for a minute, then nodded. "Okay. Apology accepted. But don't fuck with me like that ever again, Ian, do you understand me?" He leaned forward and stuck a finger in Ian's face.

Ian stepped back and raised his hands, saying with a nervous smile. "Woah, hey! Yeah, I understand. Promise. Okay." He tittered nervously then turned to approach the area where he had set up his cameras and lights. He instructed some actors to get across the room and get ready, then continued to set up the scene.

Three actors approached Charlie, their cocks swinging between their legs as they strolled across the bar. Charlie knelt on the uneven wooden floor and began to service them. He ran his tongue over each dick then began to suck, working the other two with his hands while he was administering to one. The men talked about the awards ceremony and the parties that had followed.

"Okay, Steven and Troy," Ian called. "We're ready for you."

Two men turned away from Charlie and headed back across the room to begin their scene. The last actor sighed and leaned back against a pool table. "That feels really nice."

Charlie dropped the dick from his mouth and looked up with a smile. "Thanks, that's good to hear." The actor looked familiar, but Charlie did not know his name.

A few minutes later the third actor was called over and Charlie went to the restroom to rinse out his mouth. He was thirsty, but was afraid of going behind the bar to look for a bottle of water in case he might knock something over. Instead he sat on a barstool and watched the scene progress.

Two of the actors were kneeling before the third, each of them running his lips and tongue along the swollen length of his cock. One of the actors ducked down to suck the standing man's balls and the other kneeling actor opened his mouth to suck the man's cock. The full length of the shaft slid in and out of the actor's mouth, his spit making it shine beneath the lights.

As the second actor sucked the standing man's balls, he reached out with his right hand and took hold of the actor kneeling beside him and began stroking his cock. Using his left hand on himself, he increased the speed and force of his grip as they each licked and sucked at the man standing above them.

After several minutes of watching the action, Charlie's thirst won out and he moved carefully behind the bar. He was very aware of the glass bottles sitting on glass shelves in front of the large mirror to his right. He opened the coolers beneath the bar until he found the water bottles. He grabbed one, but the plastic surface was wet and it squirted out of his hands to bounce across the floor behind the bar and roll to a stop by the cash register.

"Dammit," Charlie hissed. He looked around, but no on had noticed him. He crouched down to pick up the bottle and banged his head on the bottom of the register as he straightened up. The machine, off balance in the first place, toppled to the floor with a resounding crash and busted open. Change and bills spilled out over the floor with a clatter.

"Oh for God's sake!" Ian cried. He rushed over and leaned across the bar to assess the damage, then looked up at Charlie. "How have you managed to live this long?"

Charlie shrugged. "Just lucky, I guess."

After helping clean up the mess, he sat at the bar and watched the scenes as the movie progressed. When he was needed, he knelt on the floor and serviced the actors, all the while keeping one eye on Ian to track his whereabouts in case he should get the idea to film his fluffing once again.

Around lunch time the door opened and blinding light filled the room. Charlie blinked and turned away from the intruder to shield his eyes. He felt like a nocturnal creature forced from its den at high noon. A rustle of plastic bags approached and finally settled on the bar beside him and he turned around to find Rock Harding standing next to him with a smile. He had placed several bags of Mexican take out on the bar.

"Hungry?"

Charlie grinned. "How did you know where I was?"

Rock shrugged. "I have my ways." He looked over at Ian and the actors. "I'll put their food over in that area so we can eat alone."

Charlie devoured the burritos and tacos Rock had supplied, talking and laughing with the man. They sat facing each other on bar stools, their knees sometimes touching when one or the other of them turned to grab more food. Each point of contact with Rock made Charlie's spine tingle and his stomach clench. How could one man have such an effect on him?

After lunch, Charlie had to work for an hour to get the cast ready for the shoot. When he straightened up and wiped his mouth he could feel Rock's eyes on him. He turned and looked at him openly, a smile on his face. "Are you supervising?"

Rock nodded, his eyes serious. "Yeah. And I made some notes."

Charlie climbed up on the barstool, nearly toppled off and was saved by Rock. He smiled thankfully, a little embarrassed, and adjusted himself on the cushion. "Well, when's my review?"

Rock grinned and lowered his eyes. "Well, let me put it this way: I need to supervise you for a little longer before I feel I'll be ready to go over my notes."

Charlie nodded, disappointed. "I see. Any special reason or just the most obvious one?"

"There are many reasons and I despise them all." Rock patted Charlie's knee. "I hope we can still be friends until that day."

"I think we can." Charlie took a breath and watched him stand up. "Take care. I'll see you around the sets, huh?"

Rock smiled. "You can count on it." With a wave of his hand, Rock turned and left the bar.

That evening, Charlie arrived home and collapsed on his futon. What a day! He had been in The Bronco for six hours, Rock had brought lunch and basically told him where things lay, and when he had finally left the bar his eyes had nearly been seared out of his head by the light of day. But Ian had given him a generous tip, considering the damage he had done to the cash register, and he had been able to spend time with Rock. That was always a plus.

Charlie dozed off only to be awakened thirty minutes later by a pounding on his door. He staggered across the room and opened it to find Brent wearing just shorts and running shoes, his hands on his knees as he gasped for breath.

"Oh my God!" Charlie exclaimed, suddenly fully awake. "What's wrong?"

Brent waved his hand and doubled over to cough. He straightened up. "Jogging."

Charlie sighed and shook his head. "You scared the hell out of me."

Brent smiled, then tried to slow his breathing. "Come over to my place."

Charlie gave him a look. "Why?"

Brent grinned. "For fun. Come on. I'll take a shower and we can give you some practice."

Charlie followed Brent across the hall to his apartment. The hairy man shucked his running shorts off, then his sweaty jock strap and dropped them at Charlie's feet. "Try not to sniff them too much while I'm showering."

He disappeared into the bathroom and Charlie heard the shower start up. Picking up the clothing, he warily sniffed at the damp material, then buried his nose in the crotch of the jock strap. The man's odor filled his nostrils and shot to his groin. Charlie's cock began to twitch at the thought of Brent's damp, sweaty crotch.

The phone rang, startling him, and he glanced toward the bathroom. Brent was whistling in the shower, oblivious to the call. Charlie moved toward the phone, but saw the answering machine was on and left it alone. Following Brent's recorded greeting and a beep, Charlie listened to Rock Harding's voice rumble through the tiny speaker.

"Brent, it's Rock. I really think you should take the money. After all, we had a deal when you moved in the building. You did a good job of protecting Charlie and I appreciate it. I'm glad you were able to watch over him. Give me a call and we'll talk about it. Bye."

Charlie was dumbfounded. Rock had hired Brent to protect him? From whom? Cedric? And why had Brent refused Rock's money?

The shower shut off and Charlie jumped. He moved quickly across the room, feeling guilty for having overheard the message, and sat on Brent's couch. The sweaty shorts and jockstrap dangled from his hands as he stared at the floor.

"Well, thanks for picking those up." Brent leaned nude in the doorway, one hand twisting a nipple and the other absently pulling on his dick. "How about we use them in the bedroom?"

Charlie looked around. "You have a bedroom?"

Brent led him through a door to a tastefully decorated bedroom. They kissed at the foot of the bed, then Brent pulled Charlie's clothes off and stretched him out over the mattress. Opening a drawer by the bed, Brent pulled out thin leather straps and began wrapping them around Charlie's wrists.

"What are you doing?" Charlie asked nervously.

"Trust me." Brent smiled at him then lifted one wrist over Charlie's head and tied the strap to his headboard. He repeated the process to Charlie's other arm until both wrists were bound up above his head. Brent then used longer cord to tie up Charlie's ankles so that he was lying spread eagle on the center of the mattress.

"Brent, I'm not really comfortable with this . . ."

Brent stopped up Charlie's mouth with the sweat soaked jock strap then kissed his overflowing lips. He left the room for a moment and returned with a bowl of ice cubes. Putting a cube in his mouth, Brent leaned down and ran the edge of the ice over Charlie's nipples and torso as the fluffer writhed beneath him.

Moving lower, Brent took Charlie's hardening cock into his mouth and used his tongue to run the ice cube along the shaft. Charlie groaned through the jock strap. He closed his eyes and squirmed on the mattress, his motions driving his cock deeper into Brent's cold mouth.

Brent used a cube of ice on each leg and slid one around the rim of Charlie's asshole. With a grin that made Charlie's heart beat double time, Brent inserted a cube up into Charlie's puckered sphincter. The cube melted quickly, leaving the hole slick with water. Brent slid a finger up inside Charlie and stroked his prostate as he sucked the man's cock. Charlie grunted into the dirty jock strap and thrust his pelvis up off the mattress, banging his cock into Brent's face.

After taking the brunt of Charlie's thrusts for several minutes, Brent raised his head and spit down onto the glistening red shaft. He wrapped his fingers around the throbbing flesh and began to pump his fist along its length. Charlie moaned and bucked his hips, fucking Brent's fist.

Just when he thought Charlie might cum, Brent released his grip and moved up to Charlie's nipples. Charlie made an angry sound through the jock strap, causing Brent to grin as he sucked Charlie's tit.

Moving onto the bed, Brent shifted around to plant his ass over Charlie's nose and mouth. He moved his hips forward and back, rubbing his asshole and perineum over Charlie's face. With his hips in motion, Brent leaned down to begin sucking Charlie's cock again. Charlie's body undulated beneath Brent, his legs and arms pulling against the restraints.

Brent sat up over Charlie's face and turned to look down at him. "Do you want me to untie you?"

Charlie's eyes were glazed over with lust as he stared up at Brent. He shook his head slowly.

"Do you want me to sit on your cock?"

Charlie nodded vigorously. Brent got up and fetched a condom from his bedside table. He slid the latex down over Charlie's painfully hard dick, then smeared lube over its length. Sliding two lubricated fingers up inside himself, Brent climbed up on the bed and slowly sank down onto the spike of flesh jutting up from Charlie's groin. His eyes rolled into the back of his head as his rectal muscles parted around the invading prick.

"Oh, God," Brent said. "That dick feels so good in my ass."

Charlie groaned around the jock strap and closed his eyes. He lifted his hips and felt Brent's balls press up against his pelvis as his dick slid completely into him. They stayed that way for a few moments, their bodies connected and their eyes locked. Then Brent began to rise and fall on Charlie's cock. He reached out and pinched Charlie's nipples between his fingers, bringing the flesh up into hard bumps.

Charlie moved his hips up and brought them back down onto the mattress, sinking his cock deep into Brent's ass with each thrust.

Before long he was hammering up into the man, the wet slap of friction bringing him closer to the edge of his orgasm.

Charlie punched his hips up hard and heard a low, satisfied grunt from Brent as his cock wedged itself deeper into the man's anal cavity. Cum sprayed from Brent's stocky dick, soaking Charlie's chest and belly and spattering over his face. The sharp odor of semen filled the room and Charlie shouted into the jock strap gag as he blew his load into the tip of the condom.

Panting, the two lay on the mattress, Charlie's softening cock still nestled in Brent's ass. The bear eased himself off Charlie's dick and peeled away the condom. He wrapped it in a tissue, then pulled the jock strap from Charlie's mouth and leaned down to kiss him softly.

"That was really hot," Brent whispered.

"Incredibly hot," Charlie said. He watched Brent untie the leather straps and rubbed the slightly reddened skin. "I liked the ice trick."

"Learned that a long time ago," Brent replied. He wiped his cum off Charlie's body, then climbed into bed beside him and pulled him close. "Did you have a nice day?"

Charlie nodded, his fingers snarled in Brent's chest hair. His body was tired, but his mind began to review the message Rock had left for Brent. It had sounded like Rock had asked Brent to keep an eye on him, but for what purpose? And why couldn't Rock bring himself to leave Cedric?

Charlie yawned and snuggled in closer to Brent. All the excitement of the last few days had worn him out. He had plenty of time to figure everything out. For the moment he was going to simply enjoy himself and let tomorrow take care of itself.

Charlie fell asleep with his head on Brent's shoulder, The Hummer award sitting beneath the chili pepper lights on his entertainment center across the hall.

THE END

About the Author

Hank Edwards has had over three dozen short stories published in various gay erotic magazines including *Men, 100% Beef,* and *Honcho*, as well as a number of anthologies and web sites. He lives in Michigan with his very patient partner of many years and their two cats who hope you buy several copies of his book as they want to upgrade their kitty condo. He is currently working on two sequels to *Fluffers, Inc.*, both of which he finds erotic and charming, if he does say so himself. Visit his website at hankedwardsbooks.com.

CPSIA information can be obtained at www.ICGtesting.com
Printed in the USA
BVOW07046150713

325654BV00001B/11/P